Leonardo Padura was born in Havana in 1955 and lives in Cuba. He has published a number of novels, short-story collections and literary essays. International fame came with the Havana Quartet, all featuring Inspector Mario Conde, of which *Havana Gold* is the fourth to be available in English. The Quartet has won a number of literary prizes including the Spanish Premio Hammett. It has sold widely in Spain, France, Italy and Germany.

HAVANA GOLD

Leonardo Padura

Translated by Peter Bush

BITTER LEMON PRESS
LONDON

BITTER LEMON PRESS

First published in the United Kingdom in 2008 by
Bitter Lemon Press, 37 Arundel Gardens, London W11 2LW

www.bitterlemonpress.com

First published in Spanish as *Vientos de Cuaresma* by
Tusquets Editores S.A., Barcelona, 2001

Bitter Lemon Press gratefully acknowledges
the financial assistance of the Arts Council of England

A CIP record for this book is available from the British Library

ISBN 978-1-904738-28-2

Typeset by Alma Books Ltd
Printed and bound in the United Kingdom
By Cox & Wyman Ltd, Reading, Berkshire

For Paloma and Paco Taibo II.
And once more, as ever,
for you, Lucía.

SPRING 1989

*He is the one who knows the mystery
and bears witness . . .*

The Koran

It was Ash Wednesday and, eternally punctual, a parched, choking wind swept through the barrio stirring up filth and sorrow, as if sent straight from the desert to recall the Messiah's sacrifice. Sand from quarries and ancient hatreds stuck to rancour and fear and the rubbish overflowing from bins; the last dry leaves of winter scattered, coated with the stench from the tannery, and the birds of spring vanished as if anticipating an earthquake. The dust cloud smothered the evening light and each act of breathing required a conscious, painful effort.

From the entrance to his house, Mario Conde contemplated his barrio in the wake of that apocalyptic storm: empty streets, closed doors, cowering trees, as if ravaged by a cruel, meticulous war, and he thought how behind sealed doors hurricanes of passion might now rage as destructively as the wind on the street. He felt deep within himself the first signs of a predictable attack of thirst and melancholy, also brought on by the hot breeze. He unbuttoned his shirt and walked towards the pavement. He knew his lack of an agenda for that night and the dryness in his throat could be down to a superior a superior power, one able to channel his destiny between infinite thirst and relentless solitude. With the wind blowing in his face, the dust chafing his skin, he accepted that something accursed lurked in the gale from Armageddon that unleashed itself every spring to remind mortals of the ascension of a son of man to the most dramatic of holocausts, far off in Jerusalem.

He took deep breaths until he felt his lungs collapsing under the weight of the dirt and soot, and reckoning he'd paid his dues in suffering to his restless self-torture, he returned to the shelter of his doorway and stripped off his shirt. The parched feeling in his throat now burnt more keenly, while the certainty he was alone had run riot and was trickier to trace to any particular corner of his body. It flowed unchecked, as if coursing through his veins. "You're always bloody remembering", his friend Skinny Carlos constantly told him: Lent and loneliness inevitably meant he remembered. That wind brought to the surface the black sands and detritus in his memory, brittle leaves of dead loves and bitter odours of guilt, with an intensity more perverse than forty days in the desert. Fuck this wind, he muttered, resolving not to wallow further in his melancholy, because he knew the antidote – a bottle of rum and a woman, the more whorish the better – was the perfect, instant cure for a depression that couldn't decide whether it was located in his soul or in his skin.

10

The rum was a possibility, even within the bounds of the law, he thought. The challenge was to combine it with that likely woman he'd met three days ago who was now prompting an undertow of hope and frustration. It had all started on Sunday, after lunch at Skinny's – who was no longer Skinny – which confirmed that Josefina was in league with Lucifer. Only that butcher with the infernal nickname could foster the sin of gluttony where his friend's mother plunged them: incredible but true, an almost hundred-per-cent Madrid-style stew, the dame explained, summoning them to the dining room where bowls of stew were already in place, as was a platter, circumspect yet full of promise, overflowing with chunks of meat, juicy titbits and chickpeas.

"My mother was from Asturias, but always cooked her stews Madrid-style. A matter of taste, you know? But the downside is that along with the salted pigs' trotters, piece of chicken, bacon, sausage, black pudding, potatoes, greens and chickpeas, it should also contain green beans and a cow's knee-bone, which were the only things I couldn't get. Even so, it tastes good, you must agree?" she asked rhetorically, pleased by the sincere astonishment on the faces of her son and the Count, who flung themselves at the meal, agreeing from the first spoonful: yes, it tasted good, despite lacking the refinements lamented by Josefina.

11

"Bloody great," said one.

"Hey, leave some for the others," warned the other.

"You cunt, that chorizo was mine," protested the former.

"I'm fit to burst," confessed the latter.

After such an extraordinary lunch, eyes shut, arms weighing a ton and clamouring physically for bed, Skinny was nonetheless set on sitting in front of the television and enjoying his dessert: a double hitter of baseball. The Havana team was at last playing decently, and the scent of victory riveted him to every game his team played, even when it was only broadcast on the radio. He followed the progress of the championship with a loyalty that could only be displayed by an unredeemed optimist like himself, despite the fact they'd not won a thing since that distant year of 1976 when even baseball players seemed more romantic, genuine and happy.

"I'm fucking off," said the Count, after a yawn that shook his whole body. "And don't build your hopes up too high, savage: this lot fouls up and loses the big games – remember last year."

"It's like I always said, you beast, I love you like this: so enthusiastic and spirited . . ." and he wagged his index finger at him. "You're a scabby bastard. But this year we are going to win."

"All right, if you think so, but don't say I didn't warn you . . . In any case, I've a report to write that I keep putting off till tomorrow. Just remember I'm a prole-tarian . . ."

"Fuck off. Today's Sunday. Look, my boy, Valle and the Duke are pitching today, it's a piece of cake . . ." he added, looking at him questioningly. "You liar. You've got something else in mind."

"If only," sighed the Count, who hated placid Sunday afternoons. He'd always thought the best metaphor his writer friend Baby Face Miki had ever coined was the one about being queerer than a languid Sunday afternoon. "If only," he repeated, and stood behind the wheelchair where his friend had existed for almost ten years, steering him into the living room.

"Go on, why not buy a bottle and spend tonight here?" suggested Skinny Carlos.

"I'm skint, you savage."

"Take some money from my bedside table."

"Hey, I've got to be in work early in the morning," the Count faked a protest, following the route marked out by his friend's threatening finger to the whereabouts of the money. His yawn changed into a smile and he recognized there was no way out: I might as well give up, right? "Well, I don't know. I'll see if I can come tonight. If I can find some rum," still fighting his corner, trying to save a scrap of his dignity that was under siege. "I'm off downtown."

"Don't buy home-made gut-rot," Carlos warned and the Count shouted from the passageway: "Orientales

13

for champions!" And scarpered to avoid insults he well deserved.

He went out into the steaming early afternoon, bleary-eyed, weighing up the options. I'm right, he thought, balancing duty against peremptory bodily needs: fully aware a verdict had already been delivered in favour of a siesta as Madrid-style as the stew, he muttered, "The report or bed?" as he went round the corner to get back to the 10 October Highway. And he imagined her before she actually come into view.

The experiment rarely failed: when he boarded a bus, when he went into a shop, reached an office, or even entered a shadowy cinema, the Count went through the motions and was always pleased to corroborate its effectiveness: the deep reflexes of a trained animal always led his eyes towards the figure of the most beautiful woman in the place, as if the quest for beauty formed part of his vital needs. And that magnetic aesthetic attraction able to trigger off his libido couldn't have let him down now. In the bright sunlight the woman stood out like a vision from another world: gleaming red hair, all soft and curly; legs like Corinthian columns, climaxing in luscious hips, barely covered by frayed, cut-down jeans; her face red from the heat, half hidden by round sunglasses, above a set of fleshy lips belonging to a woman determined to enjoy life to the full. A mouth to suit any whim, fantasy or imaginable need. How tasty can you get! he muttered. It was as if she'd sprung from the rays of the sun, hot and tailor-made for his atavistic desires. The Count hadn't had an erection in the street for a long time – the years had made him slow and overly cerebral – but suddenly he felt something disruptive in his nether regions, just beneath the protean layers of Madrid stew, and the waves provoked by that movement led to an unexpected firmness between his legs. She leaned against the car's rear mudguard and, as he stared at her long-distance runner's thighs, the Count understood why she was sunbathing in the street: a flat tyre and hydraulic jack lying against the kerb explained the despair he could see on her face when she removed her glasses and wiped the sweat from her face with such elegant panache. Mustn't even let it cross my mind, the Count warned himself, predicting his usual awkwardness and timidity and, as he drew level with the woman, he greeted her as boldly as he knew how: "Can I help?"

That smile was worth any sacrifice, even the public sacrifice of a siesta. Her mouth broadened out and the Count thought that the sun had no need to shine.

"Really?" she hesitated for a moment, but only for a moment. "I just came out to get some petrol, and look what's happened," she moaned, pointing her greasy hands at the mortally wounded tyre.

"Are the nuts too tight?" he asked, by way of introduction, as he clumsily tried to look handy at putting a jack in place. She crouched down next to him, keen to express her moral solidarity, and the Count saw a bead of sweat launch itself down the lethal incline of her neck and plunge between two small breasts that were no doubt free and firm under her sweat-stained blouse. She smells like a femme fatale coming on, warned the persistent protuberance the Count tried to conceal between his legs. Well, who'd have thought it, Mario Conde?

Yet again Conde grasped why he always got low marks for manual techniques and workplace training. It took him half an hour to change the punctured wheel but in that time he discovered you tighten nuts from left to right and not right to left; that her name is Karina and she's twenty-eight, an engineer; and that she is separated and living with her mother and a half-crazy brother, a rock musician playing in the band: The Mutants. The Mutants? He'd also found out that you must use your foot to turn the nuts with the spanner, and that she was driving to Matanzas in the morning with a technical unit to work in the fertilizer factory till Friday – and, yes, it was true, she'd always lived in that house opposite, although the Count had been going down that same street every night for nigh on twenty years – and she'd even once read something by Salinger and she thinks he's fantastic (and he even thought of correcting her: no, he's squalid and moving. In short, he learned that changing a flat tyre can be one of the most exacting jobs around.

Karina's gratitude was bubbly, all embracing, when she suggested he should accompany her to get petrol and then she'd drive him home – look how sweaty you are, you've got oil on your face, oh dear, I told you – and the Count felt his little heart race at these slow, sweet words from that woman, who liked a laugh and who'd appeared from nowhere.

At the end of the afternoon, after queuing for petrol and discovering that Karina's mum had attached an Easter palm leaf to the rear-view mirror, after chattering about punctured cars, Lenten heat and winds, and drinking coffee at the Count's, they agreed she would call him as soon as she got back from Matanzas: she could return *Franny* and *Zooey*, it's the best Salinger ever wrote, the Count had remarked, unable to contain his enthusiasm, handing her a book he'd never lent anyone ever since he'd stolen it from the university library. That way, they could meet up and chat a bit more. OK?

The Count's eyes had remained glued to her and, although he recognized quite candidly that the girl wasn't as beautiful as in his first impressions (her mouth was too big, her eye-lashes fluttered rather sadly and

17

she was rather deficient in the backside department, he concluded critically) he was nonetheless impressed by her constant cheerfulness and unexpected ability, in the middle of the street, after lunch and under a murderous sun, to raise a virile extremity that had neither legs nor wings.

Karina accepted a second cup of coffee and it was now time for the revelation that would finally drive the Count mad.

"My father turned me into a coffee addict," she said looking at him. "He drank coffee all day, whatever he could get."

"And what else did he teach you?"

She smiled and swayed her head, as if chasing off ideas and memories.

"He taught me everything he knew, even how to play the saxophone."

"The saxophone?" he almost shouted, incredulously. "You can play the saxophone?"

"Well, I'm not a musician or anything like. But I do blow that horn, as jazz musicians say. He loved jazz and played with lots of people, with Frank Emilio, with Cachao, with Felipe Dulzaides, the old guard . . ."

The Count hardly heard what she said about her father and the trios, quintets and septets he'd played in over the years, the jam sessions in the Grotto, Las Vegas and Copa Room, and had no need to close his eyes to

18

imagine Karina with the sax's mouthpiece between her lips and the instrument's neck dancing between her legs. Is this woman for real? he wondered.

"What about you? Do you like jazz?"

"You know . . . it's something I can't live without," he replied opening his arms out to emphasize the depths of his passion. She smiled and appreciated his play-acting.

"OK, I must be off. I've things to get ready for tomorrow."

"So you'll ring me?" asked the Count almost imploring her.

"Of course, the moment I get back."

The Count lit a cigarette, injecting himself with smoke and Dutch courage, before he made the decisive move.

"What did you mean by 'separated'?" he blurted out, gawping like a half dopey pupil.

"Look it up in the dictionary," she retorted, smiling and swaying her head once again. She picked up her car keys and walked towards the door. The Count pursued her to the kerb. "Thanks for everything, Mario," she said and, after pondering for a moment, asked: "Hey, isn't it about time you told me about yourself?"

The Count threw his cigarette into the street and smiled as he felt he was back on safe ground.

"I'm a policeman," he replied, folding his arms, in a gesture to accompany his revelation.

Karina looked at him, nibbled her lip, then asked, disbelievingly: "Canadian Mounties or Scotland Yard? I guessed as much. You look like a liar," she said, leaning on Conde's folded arms and kissing his cheek. "Bye-bye, Mr Policeman."

Detective Lieutenant Mario Conde was still smiling after the Polish Fiat disappeared round the bend in the Highway. He trotted happily home dreaming of future bliss.

But it was still only Ash Wednesday, however much he counted and re-counted the hours to their next meeting. The three days he had to wait gave him time enough to imagine the whole works – marriage and children included, after a prior period of lovemaking on beds, beaches, tropical foliage and British meadows, in hotels of diverse constellations, on moonlit and moonless nights and dawns, in Polish Fiats – and then he'd see her, naked, sax between legs, sucking the mouthpiece, before launching into a mellow, golden melody. All he could do was imagine, wait and masturbate, as the image of Karina, sax at the ready, became unbearably erotic.

As he'd decided yet again to settle for the company of Skinny Carlos and a bottle of rum, Conde pulled on a shirt and shut the door to his house. He went out into the dust and wind on the street, muttering that, though he found Lent enervating and depressing, right then he belonged to a rare breed of policemen on the brink of great happiness.

"Aren't you fuckin' well going to tell me what you're up to?"

The Count smiled vaguely at his friend: what do I tell him? he thought. The almost three-hundred pounds of defeated body in that wheelchair creased his heart. He felt it too cruel to talk of imminent bliss with a man whose pleasures in life had been reduced forever to alcohol-powered conversations, gargantuan meals and a morbid fanaticism for baseball. Ever since he'd been shot in Angola and become a life-long invalid, Skinny Carlos, who was no longer skinny, had become a dirge, an infinite pain the Count bore with guilt-ridden stoicism. What lie shall I tell? Do I have to lie even to him? he wondered, smiling bitterly, as he saw himself walking slowly past Karina's, even stopping and trying to glimpse through the porch windows the woman's impossible presence in a shadowy room crammed with ferns and red and orange-hearted *malangas.* How come he'd never seen her, given she was the sort you scented a mile off? He downed his rum and declared: "I was going to lie."

"Do you still have to do that?"

"I don't think I am what you think I am, Skinny. I'm not the same as you."

21

"Look, guy, if you want to talk shit, just get it out," he said, lifting his hand to signal the pause necessary to knock back another rum. "I'll just put myself on fast-forward. But remember one thing: you may not be one of the wonders of this world, but you are the best friend I have in the world. Even if your lies will be the death of me."

"Savage, I met a woman out there and I think . . ." he looked Skinny in the eye.

"Fucking hell!" exclaimed Skinny Carlos, also smiling. "So that was what it was all about. You're incurable, aren't you?"

"Give me a break, Skinny, I'd like you to see her. You know, you probably have, she lives just round the corner, in the next block, her name's Karina. She's an engineer, a redhead and fantastically sexy. I can feel her right here," and he pressed his finger on the space between his eyebrows.

"Hey, you bastard, slow down . . . you're going too fast for me. Is she your latest?"

"If only," the Count sighed, looking forlorn. He poured himself more rum and recounted his meeting with Karina, down to the tiniest detail (the whole truth, even about the shortfall in her rear, knowing full well how highly a good rump rated in Skinny's aesthetic judgements), and his future expectations (even the adolescent spying from the street he'd practised that night). In the end he always told his friend the whole story, however happy or wretched it might be.

The Count saw Skinny stretch but not reach the bottle and gave it to him. The level of liquid was already down behind the label and he calculated that theirs was a two-litre conversation, but hunting for rum in La Víbora at that hour of the night would be a futile, desperate business. The Count regretted that reality: talking about Karina, in Skinny's room, surrounded by tangible nostalgia and posters that had faded with time, he was beginning to feel as relaxed as in the old days, when their whole world had turned on good rum, firm tits and, above all, the magnetic, magical orifice they always referred to in terms of its lushness, depth, hairiness and ease of access (Oh no, guy, look at the way she walks, if she's a virgin, I'm a helicopter, Skinny would say), not worrying a bit about who owned those limpid objects of desire.

"You don't change, you bastard, you know fuck all about that woman, but you're already like a horny mongrel. Look what happened to you with Tamara . . ."

"Hey, man, don't compare . . ."

"No shit, you're . . . So she lives just round the corner? You're not just dreaming this up?"

"No, I kid you not. You know, Skinny, I've just got to lay that woman. Either I lay her or kill myself, go mad or turn queer."

"Better queer than dead," his friend interjected smiling.

"Too true, savage. My life's gone flat. I need a woman like her. I don't know anything about her, but I need her."

Skinny looked at him as if to say: You're incurable.

"I don't know, but I've a hunch you're talking shit again . . . You like rubbing salt in the wound . . . You're a policeman because it's what you fucking want to be. If you don't, then get out, and damn everything else . . . But then don't come telling me you really liked pissing on bastards and arseholes. I can't stand any more of your bellyaching. What happened to you with Tamara was already written in blood, my friend: she was never a dame for fellows like us, so forget her once and for all and make a note in your autobiography that at least you took out the sting and gave her a good fuck. And shit on the world, you savage. Come on, a drop more of the juice."

The Count looked at the bottle and regretted the end was nigh. He needed to hear from Skinny's mouth the things he himself was thinking, and tonight, while the Lenten wind stirred up filth outside, while hope flickered deep down in the form of woman, being in his best friend's bedroom, speaking about everything under the sun, both cleansed and encouraged him. What will I do if Skinny dies on me? he wondered, breaking the chain that led to spiritual peace. He opted for suicide via alcohol: poured out more rum for his friend, gave himself another shot and realized they'd forgotten to talk about baseball or listen to music. Let's go for music, he decided.

He got up and opened the drawer with the cassettes. As usual, he was appalled by Skinny's mix of musical tastes: anything went, from the Beatles and the Mustangs, to Joan Manuel Serrat and Gloria Estefan.

"What do you want to hear?"

"The Beatles?"

"Chicago?"

"Formula V?"

"Los Pasos?"

"Credence?"

"Huh-huh, Credence . . . But don't say Tom Foggerty sings like a black, I've told you he sings like God, haven't I?" And they both nodded their heartfelt agreement: the bastard sings like God.

The bottle expired well before the long version of *Proud Mary*. Skinny put his glass on the floor and moved his wheelchair to the edge of the bed where his friend the policeman was seated. He placed one of his spongy hands on Conde's shoulder and looked him in the eye: "I hope it turns out OK for you, my brother. Good guys deserve a bit more luck in life."

The Count thought how right he was: Skinny himself was the best person he knew and luck had not run his

25

way. But he felt that was all far too pathetic and tried to smile, retorting: "You're the one talking shit now, guy. The good guys had their day long ago."

And he got up wanting to give his friend a hug, but didn't dare. There were hundreds and hundreds of things he never dared do.

Nobody can imagine what night-time is like for a policeman. Nobody can know what ghosts visit him, what hot flushes assail him, the hell where he simmers on a slow burner or where fierce flames shoot around him. The act of closing your eyes can be a cruel challenge, conjuring up troublesome figures from the past, who never leave your memory, who return, night after night, with the tireless regularity of a pendulum. Decisions, mistakes, acts of arrogance, even the frailties of generosity return like irredeemable sins to haunt a conscience marked by each petty act of infamy committed in the world of the infamous. José de la Caridad sometimes pays me a visit, that black truck driver who asked, begged me not to send him to jail because he was innocent, and I questioned him over four days, it just had to be him, it couldn't be anyone else, as he collapsed and wept and repeated his innocence, until I put him behind bars to await a trial that found him innocent. Sometimes Estrellita Rivero returns, the girl I tried to hold back for a second before she took that fatal step and was shot between the eyes by Sergeant Mateo who'd meant to hit the legs of the man running away. Or Rafael and Tamara waltzing out of death or the past, as if it were twenty years ago, he in a suit and she in a long white dress, like the bride she was soon to be. Nothing is gentle in the night of a policeman, not even the memory of that last woman or the hope of the next, because each memory and each hope – that will one day be a memory – is tarnished by the daily horrors in his life: I met her while investigating the death of her husband, the frauds, lies, bribes, abuses and fears of that man who seemed perfect from the heights of his power; I'll remember her, perhaps, because of someone's murder, another's rape or sorrow. A policeman's nights are murky waters: they reek foul and bear the colour of death. To sleep! . . . Perchance to dream! And I have learned there is only one way to defeat them: lack of consciousness, dying a little every day, and every dawn is death itself, when what should be joyful sunshine is torture to the eyes. Horror at the past, fear of the future: that's how a policeman's nights rush towards daytime. To catch, question, imprison, judge, sentence, accuse, repress, persecute, pressurize and crush are the verbs which conjugate the memories and entire life of a policeman. I dream I could dream other happy dreams, build something, possess something, hand something on, receive and create something: write. But it's the futile delirium of a man who feeds on what has been destroyed. That is why a policeman's loneliness is the most fearful loneliness: it accompanies his ghosts, sorrows, guilt . . . If only a woman would play a lullaby on her saxophone to send this particular policeman to sleep. But, silence, only silence! Night has fallen. Outside an accursed wind ravages the earth.

The two analgesics weighed on his stomach like a great burden of guilt. Conde had swallowed them in a huge cup of black coffee, after noting that the remains of the last milk he'd purchased had become a pungent whey at the bottom of a litre bottle. Luckily he'd discovered he'd still two clean shirts in his wardrobe and had the luxury of choice: he voted for the white and brown striped option with long sleeves he rolled back to his elbow. His jeans – that had finished up under his bed – had endured a mere fortnight's campaign and could resist another fifteen or twenty days. He tucked his pistol into his trouser waistband and felt he'd lost weight, though he decided it was no cause for worry: he wasn't hungry, or cancerous, for heaven's sake. Besides, apart from his stomach ache, everything was fine: he didn't have bags under his eyes, his incipient baldness was hardly rampant, his liver was valiantly bearing up, his headache was fading and it was Thursday and tomorrow would be Friday, he counted on his fingers. He stepped into the sun and the wind and almost started leathering out an old love song.

More than a thousand years will pass, many more,
I don't know if love is eternal,
but here as much as there . . .

He walked into headquarters at eight-fifteen, greeted various colleagues, enviously read the new 1989 statement on retirement on the noticeboard in the lobby and, smoking his fifth cigarette of the day, waited for the lift in order to report to the duty officer. He was cherishing the fond hope he wouldn't be given a new case yet: he wanted to devote his intellect to a single idea, and, over the last few days he'd even felt a renewed desire to write. He'd re-read a couple of books that always got his grey cells working, and written down a few of the lines obsessing him in an old school notebook, on green-lined yellow paper, like a forgotten pitcher sent to warm his arm up before making the decisive throw. His meeting with Tamara, a few months ago, had disturbed past nostalgias, forgotten feelings and hatred he thought had disappeared and that now rushed back into his life summoned by that surprise re-encounter with a vital slice of his past he really must come to terms with, absorb or send packing once and for all. He was thinking how all that might contain material to weave a really moving story about the times when they were all very young, very poor and very happy: when Skinny was still skinny and Andrés was still set on being a baseball player, Dulcita had yet to go, Rabbit was all geared up to be a historian, naturally, Tamara had yet to marry Rafael and was so very beautiful, and even he dreamed more than ever he would be a writer and only a writer – while from his bed he contemplated the photo of old Hemingway on his wall and tried to catch the mystery behind the look in the writer's eyes which lay bare the world and saw what other eyes never saw. He thought that if he ever wrote a chronicle of love, hatred, happiness and frustration, he would call it *Havana Blue*.

The lift stopped on the third floor and the Count turned right. The floors of headquarters were gleaming, recently swept with sawdust soaked in kerosene, and the sun shone through the high glass and aluminium windows to reveal the long corridor in all its newly awakened brightness. It was so clean and well-lit it really didn't seem like a police headquarters. He pushed the double glass door and entered the room of the duty officer who was experiencing the most frantic moments in his day: officers handing in reports, detectives protesting about a court sentence, assistants in need of assistance and even Lieutenant Mario Conde, with a bolero perpetually on his lips: "From my life, I give you the best / I'm so poor what else have I to give . . ." and a cigarette between his fingers, who, as he approached the duty officer's desk, that morning occupied by Lieutenant Fabricio whose comments he barely heard: "The major wants to see you. Don't ask me what it's about. I haven't a clue and it's hell here today, and you know you get your cases from the boss, because you're his pretty boy for some reason or other."

The Count glanced at Lieutenant Fabricio: he seemed really at sea among the paperwork, ringing telephones and shouting, and he realized his hands had started to sweat; it was the second time Fabricio had treated him like that and the Count told himself there was no way he was going to tolerate his stupid jibes. A few months ago, during the investigation of a series of thefts in various Havana hotels, Major Rangel had ordered the Count to take over the case from Fabricio. The Count had tried to refuse but couldn't: the Boss had made his mind up. There was no putting him off and he had apologized to Lieutenant Fabricio, explaining that the decision wasn't his. Several days later, when the Count caught the thieves and tried to tell Fabricio how the case had ended the latter retorted: "I'm so happy for you, Conde, I bet the Major will give you a kiss at the very least". And he had looked for every possible excuse to forgive the lieutenant's attitude. And in the end had forgiven him. But now a lingering awareness of his roots reminded him he'd been born in a barrio that was too hot and unruly, where you couldn't lower the banner of manhood for a single moment, on pain of becoming bereft of banner, manhood, even of the flagpole itself: no, at his age he wasn't going to brook that kind of response. He raised a finger, prepared to launch into a spiel, and then held back. He waited for a moment until the office was empty, rested his hands on the edge of the desk, lowered his head until it was level with Fabricio's eyes and said: "Let me know if you've got an itch. I can scratch you when you want, where you want and how you want, do you get me?" And turned half round, and felt the daggers from the other man's eyes stab his back. What the fuck's wrong with the fellow . . .

That's spoilt my bloody morning, he muttered. He no longer had the patience to wait for the lift, so he attacked the stairs to the seventh floor. He felt the analgesics burden his stomach once again and thought how all that would end badly. Fuck, he told himself, he'll get what's coming to him, and went into the anteroom to Major Rangel's office.

Maruchi looked at him, nodding in his direction as she carried on with her typing.

"What's up, treasure?" he greeted her in turn, walking over to her desk.

"He sent for you really early. But apparently you'd already left," said the girl, as she nodded towards the office door. "I'm not sure but I think there's big trouble brewing."

The Count sighed and lit a cigarette. He shook when-ever the major spoke of big trouble sent from on high: Conde, you get a move on. But this time he wouldn't agree to replace anyone, even if it cost him his job. He pushed back his pistol that was always trying to flee the waistband of his jeans, more so now he was getting thinner for no apparent reason, and put a hand on the paper the Boss's secretary was copying.

"What do you reckon, Maruchi?"

The young woman looked at him and smiled.

"Are you about to declare your love after testing the terrain?"

Now it was the Count's turn to smile at his gauche behaviour: "No, it's just that even I can't stand myself right now," and he rapped his knuckles on the glass panel.

"Go on, in you come."

Major Rangel was smoking his cigar and just by its smell the Count knew that it wasn't a good day for the Boss: it reeked of a cheap, dry smoke, a sixty-cent effort, and that could definitively sour the mood of the head of headquarters. Despite the bad weed that could put a frown on his chief's face, the Count admired his martial air: he wore with distinction a uniform that showed off the bronzed tan of a squash player and daily swimmer. The bastard keeps himself fit.

"They said . . ." he started to explain, but the major

pointed him to a chair and gestured to him to keep quiet.

"Take a seat, the party's over. Get hold of Manolo because you're on a case. You're not down for anything special for a week, are you?"

The Count looked for a moment at the window in the chief's office. All he could see was a blue horizon and none of the swirling leaves and paper unleashed by the wind, and he understood there was no way out. The major was trying to revive the embers of his cigar and the distress caused by the unrequited smoker's stress was evident in every twitch of his face. The Boss wasn't at all happy that morning.

It's as if the end of the world were nigh, or we've been cursed, or people have gone mad on this island. You know, Conde: either I'm getting old or things are changing and no one bothered to inform me. I think I'm going to give up the habit, you can't smoke this stuff, just look, call this shit a cigar? Go on, take a look: the surface is more wrinkled than my grandma's arse, it's like smoking a bunch of banana leaves, it really is. I'm going to make an appointment to see a psychologist today, I'll lie him down on the couch and tell him to help me give up smoking. And yet I really need a good cigar today: I don't mean a Rey del Mundo or a Gran Corona or a Davidoff . . . I'd settle for a Montecristo . . . Maruchi,

34

bring us a cup of coffee, be so good . . . See if I can get rid of the taste of this muck. Right, if this is coffee, get God to come and vouch for it . . . Anyway, to the point. I need you to get stuck into this case and be on your best behaviour, Conde. I don't want you moaning and groaning, or going on the bottle; I want it solved now. Work with Manolo and whoever you want, you've got carte blanche but get on with it. Listen hard, this is between the two of us: something big is in the offing and I don't want us to be caught napping or in a daydream. It must be something big and ugly because I don't know the people pushing it. It's coming from very high up and heads will fly: Get this into yours right? . . . And don't ask me because I'm not in the know, you understand? Look, here's the paperwork to do with the case. But don't start reading now, my friend. I can sum up: a twenty-four-year-old high school teacher, single and a member of the Communist Youth; killed, strangled with a towel, first beaten every which way, a broken rib and a finger with a double fracture and raped by at least two men. They didn't take anything of value, apparently: neither clothes nor electrical goods . . . and traces of a joint were found in the water in the lavatory pan. Like the sound of it? It's dynamite, and I, Antonio Rangel Valdés, want to know what happened to that young woman, because I've not been a policeman for thirty years for the pure pleasure of it. There must be a lot of dirt swept under the carpet for them to kill her like that, torture, marijuana and a gang bang . . . But what kind of a cigar do you call this? It's as if the end of the world were nigh, I swear by my mother, it is. And remember what I said: behave yourself, people aren't in the mood for any of your pranks . . .

The Count thought he had a good nose for aromas. It was his only attribute he considered to be in reasonable working order and his sense of smell told him the Boss was right: that whole business reeked of shit. So much was obvious from the moment he opened the door to the flat and inspected a crime scene that only lacked the victim and her assailants. The silhouette of the young murdered teacher in her final position had been marked out in chalk: one arm had come to rest very close to her body and the other seemed to be trying to reach her head, while her legs were folded up tight against her torso in a vain effort to protect a stomach that had already been battered. It was a gruesome sight, between a sofa and the central table that had been yanked to one side.

He went into the flat and shut the door behind him, then inspected the rest of the room: an inevitably Japanese colour television and twin-deck cassette recorder with a tape, which had come to a finish on the A side, stood on a multi-use piece of furniture filling the entire wall opposite the balcony; he pressed STOP, took out the tape and read: *Private dancer,* Tina Turner. Above the television, on the longest shelf, was a line of books he found more interesting: several chemistry textbooks, Lenin's *Complete Works* in three faded red volumes, a history of Greece and a few novels that the Count would never dare read again: *Doña Barbara, Old Goriot, Mare Nostrum, Las inquietudes de Shanti Andía, Cecilia Valdés* and, at the far end, the only book he felt like stealing: *Poesía*, Pablo Neruda, that so matched his mood at that moment. He opened the book and read a few lines at random . . .

Take my bread, if you wish
take the air, but
don't take your smile . . .

. . . then put it back, because he'd got the same edition at home. She doesn't seem a very keen reader, he concluded, shaking the dust off his hands.

He walked to the balcony and opened the shutters: the light flooded in, the wind blew and a copper mobile, that the Count hadn't noticed before, started rattling. By the side of the outline chalked on the floor he spotted another silhouette, a smaller patch that had almost disappeared, staining the bright shiny tiles. Why did they kill you? he wondered as he imagined the girl raped, beaten, tortured and strangled, lying in her own blood.

He went into the only bedroom in the flat and found the bed made up. A poster of an almost beautiful Barbra Streisand from the time of *The Way We Were* had been carefully framed and hung on one wall. On the other side was a huge mirror the usefulness of which the Count decided to test; he flopped on the bed and saw himself full-length. Wonderful, wasn't it? Then he opened the wardrobe and his initial reaction to the scent gathered strength: it wasn't a normal or ordinary selection of clothes: blouses, smocks, trousers, pullovers, shoes, knickers and overcoats, the Count noted, with their made-in-some-far-off-place labels.

He went back into the living room and looked out from the balcony. That fourth floor in Santos Suárez had a privileged view of a city which from that height looked especially decrepit, dirty, unapproachable and hostile. He noticed several pigeon lofts on the flat roofs and a few dogs sunbathing in the sun and wind and identified jerry-built additions to the rooftops, stuck like fish-scales to rooms that now housed entire families; he contemplated water tanks open to the dust and rain, rubbish abandoned in dangerous places, and breathed out when he saw opposite a small roof garden made out of milk churns that had been sawn in half and planted with shrubs and flowers. It was then he realized that Skinny's house was to his right, just over a mile away behind clumps of trees that blocked his view, and, round the corner, Karina's – and he again reminded himself it was Thursday already.

He went back into the living room and sat down as far away as possible from the chalk figure. He opened the report the Boss had given him and, as he read, told himself that it was sometimes worthwhile being a policeman.

Who was this Lissette Núñez Delgado?

Lissette Núñez Delgado would have been twenty-five in December, in that year of 1989. She had been born in Havana in 1964, when the Count was nine, wore orthopaedic shoes and was in his full childhood glory as a street urchin, one who'd never imagined for a single minute – and never would for the next fifteen years – that he'd become a policeman and have occasion to investigate the death of that girl born in a modern flat in the district of Santos Suárez. The young woman graduated two years ago with a chemistry degree from the Havana Higher Institute for Teaching and, contrary to what one might expect in that era of vacancies in the rural schools of the island's interior, was immediately allocated to the Pre-University High School in La Víbora – the very same where the Count studied between 1972 and 1975 and made friends with Skinny Carlos. The fact she was a teacher at the Víbora Pre-Uni could count against her: almost everything related to that place aroused the Count's fond nostalgia or implacable rejection. Lissette's father had died three years ago and her mother, who'd divorced him in 1970, lived in Casino Deportivo, in the house belonging to her second husband, a high-ranking civil servant in the Ministry of Education – a position that explained why the young girl hadn't done her social service outside Havana. Her mother, a journalist on the magazine *Rebel Youth*, was more or less renowned thanks to her opportune articles, that ranged from fashion and cooking to attempts to convince her readers, through examples from everyday life, of her ethical and political muscle, and of the fact she was an ideological role model. Her image was bolstered by frequent television appearances, when she held forth on hairstyles, make-up and home decoration, "because beauty and happiness are possible", she would say. Quite coincidentally, Conde had always reacted to this woman Caridad Delgado as if she were a kick in the gut: she seemed hollow and tasteless, a fruit sucked dry. As for her deceased father he had been a lifelong bureaucrat: from glass factories to costume-jewellery companies, via meat plants, the Coppelia ice-creamery and a bus terminal, which brought on a massive heart attack.

Lissette had been a member of the Youth from the age of sixteen and her ideological record sheet seemed pristine: not a single caution or minor sanction. How come she never had a slip of memory, never made a slight error of judgement or swore at anybody? She'd been a leading cadre in the Pioneers, the School and University Student Federations, and although the report mentioned nothing specific she must have participated fully in the activities programmed by these organizations. She earned 198 pesos a month because she was still in the so-called period of Social Service, paid twenty in rent, was docked eighteen a month for the refrigerator voted to her in a mass meeting and must have spent around thirty on lunch, afternoon snack and transport to Pre-Uni. Were 130 pesos enough to assemble that wardrobe? Recent fingerprints from five people had been found at her place, not including hers, but none was on file. Her third-floor neighbour was the only one who'd said anything at all useful: he heard music and rhythmic dancing the night of her death, 19 March 1989. End of report.

The photo of Lissette accompanying the report didn't look very up-to-date: it had gone dark round the edges and the face of the young girl caught there forever didn't look very attractive, despite the fact her eyes were deep set and sultry, with thick eyebrows that might have given her one of those so-called enigmatic looks. If I'd have known you . . . Standing up, leaning against the balcony rail again, the Count watched the sun rise determinedly to its zenith; he saw a woman struggling against the wind to hang out her washing on a flat roof; he saw a young

41

boy in school uniform climbing up wooden stairs to a roof where he opened the door of a pigeon loft and released several racing pigeons – they disappeared into the distance, beating their liberated wings against stormy gusts; and saw, on a third floor, on the other side of the street, a scene that kept him on edge for a few minutes, stunned by the shock of those who peep at private acts. Next to a window, open to the Lenten winds, a man in his forties and a possibly slightly younger woman were arguing. Although their shouts vanished in the wind, the Count saw the threats from fists and nails grow as the two bodies edged closer towards each other, on fire, ready to explode. Conde felt caught by that escalating tragedy reaching silently out to him: he saw her hair flap like a flag unfurled by the wind, while his face reddened with every gust. It's that accursed wind, he muttered, as the woman went over to the window and closed the shutters forcing the peeping tom to imagine the finale. While the Count was thinking the man was surely in the right – she was acting like a wild animal – he saw a car lurch crazily round the corner, its rubber-burning tyres screeching to a halt in front of the building where Lissette Núñez Delgado lived. The car-door opened and a lanky, ill-built Sergeant Manuel Palacios stepped out, his work-colleague yet again: Sergeant Palacios gave a smile of satisfaction when he looked up and discovered Conde could now include that display of Formula One driving in a Lada 1600 among the many things he had seen.

It can't be true, he muttered. His nostalgia couldn't still be at the old levels. From the perspective of 1989, it now acted like a cloying, scented sensation that was soothingly authentic and embraced him with the decanted passion of vintage loves. Conde had prepared himself for an attack of aggressive nostalgia that would call him to account and claim back the interest that had mounted up over the years, but the prolonged wait had served to smooth all of memory's rough edges, to leave only that peaceful feeling of belonging to a place and a time veiled by a rose-tinted selectivity that wisely and nobly preferred to evoke moments beyond rancour, hatred and sadness. Yes, I can resist, he thought, gazing at the square columns that supported the lofty entrance to La Víbora's old Secondary Education School – later transformed into the Pre-Uni that would be the refuge, for three years, of the dreams and hopes of that hidden generation that longed to be so much that never was. The shadow from the ancient *majaguas* with their red and yellow flowers climbed the short stairway, blotting out the midday sun, even protecting the bust of Carlos Manuel de Céspedes who wasn't what he used to be either: the classic figure from the old days, head, neck and shoulders cast in bronze, edged in green by repeated downpours, had been replaced by an ultra-modern image seemingly buried in a big block of badly set concrete. It can't be true, he repeated, because he desperately wanted it to be an illusion, wanted life to be a rehearsal you could improve on before the final performance: Skinny Carlos, when he was very skinny with two healthy legs that walked, ran and jumped through that entrance and down those steps with the joy of the righteous, while his friend the Count stared at all the girls who wouldn't be his girlfriends however deeply he desired them; Andrés who suffered (as only he could) the pain of love; and Rabbit, as parsimonious as ever, who intended to change the world by refashioning history from a precise moment – which might be the victory of the Arabs in Poitiers, of Moctezuma over Cortés or, simply, the English staying on in Havana after taking the city in 1762 . . . Their childhood had died a death between those columns, in those classrooms, behind those stairs and on that square illogically dubbed "red" when it was black, simply black, like everything else stained by the soot and grease from the nearby bus stop. Although they'd only learned a few mathematical equations and stubbornly invariable laws of physics, they'd become adults as they grasped the meaning of betrayal and evil, saw climbers climb and a few sincere souls experience frustration, fell passionately in love, got drunk on joy and sorrow, and discovered, above all, their absolute need for what goes by the name

44

of friendship for want of a better . . . No, it's not untrue. It was worth experiencing the distress of that unexpectedly benign nostalgia, if only as a tribute to friendship, he convinced himself, as he walked between the columns and listened to Manolo explain to the caretaker on the door that they wanted to see the headmaster.

The caretaker looked at Conde and Conde looked at the caretaker and, for a second, the policeman felt he'd been caught in the act. An elegant man with stylish hair, well into his sixties, his bright eyes sparkled at the lieutenant with an I-know-him-from-somewhere look. Perhaps if Manolo hadn't introduced him as a policeman, the caretaker might have asked if he wasn't the little bastard who used to escape his clutches every day at twelve-fifteen by jumping over the wall in the PE yard.

A gentle buzz reached them from the classrooms and the inside playground was empty. The Count decided conclusively that this place, where he'd now returned after an absence of fifteen years, wasn't the one he had left. Perhaps his memory did retain the unmistakeable smell of chalk dust and the alcoholic aroma of stencils, but not that reality intent on confusing him by distorting every dimension: what he thought would be small turned out to be too big, as if it had burgeoned in the intervening years, and what he thought would be huge turned out to be insignificant or non-existent, since it perhaps existed only in his most emotional memories. They walked through the secretariat to the headmaster's office, and he found it impossible not to remember the day when he'd followed the same route to hear himself accused of writing idealist stories which defended religion. Fuck the lot of you, he'd almost shouted, when a young woman came out of the headmaster's office and asked them why they'd come.

"We would like to speak to the headmaster. Our visit is related to the case of the teacher Lissette Núñez Delgado."

"It's often said that teaching is an art, and there's a lot of literature and fine words written about education. But the truth is that the philosophy of teaching is one thing, while exercising it every day, year in year out, is quite another. I do apologize. I can't even offer you a cup of coffee. Or tea. But please do sit down. What people don't say is that you must be rather mad to teach. Do you know what it's like to manage a Pre-Uni high school? Better you don't, for it's just that, madness. I don't know what's happening but young people are less and less interested in really learning. Do you know how long I've been in this trade? Twenty-six years, my dear colleagues, twenty-six: I started as a schoolmaster, and now I've been a head for fifteen and I think it only goes from bad to worse. Something's not working properly, and if the truth be told, young people now are quite different. It's

46

as if the world was suddenly going too fast. Yes, it must be something like that. They say it's a symptom of post-modern society. So we too can be called postmodern in this heat and our jam-packed buses? The fact is I leave here with a headache every day. I don't mind the fact they're obsessed with their hair, shoes and clothes, or that they all want to be shafting like crazy at the age of fifteen if you'll excuse my French, because that's all quite predictable, isn't it? But at least they could care a little bit about their schooling. Every year we expel a number who have all but dropped out of society and, according to their lights, drop-outs don't study, work or make demands: they only want to be left in peace, you know, to be left in peace to make love not war. Just like the good old Sixties, you see? . . . But what most upsets me is that if you get hold of a twelfth grader now, with only three months to go to graduation, and ask him what he's going to study, he won't know, and if he does, he won't know why. They're eternally adrift . . . But do excuse my harangue. Luckily, you aren't from the Ministry of Education, are you? Yesterday morning we were paid a visit and told about dear comrade Lissette. I really find it hard to believe. It's hard to get your head round the fact that a young person who you'd see looking healthy and cheerful every day is now dead. Yes, she started here with the tenth grade, and, to tell the truth, neither I nor her head of department had any complaints: she did everything demanded of her and did it well. I think she's one of the few young people to come to us with a real vocation to be a teacher. She liked her work and was always coming up with ideas to motivate her pupils. She could just as easily go camping with them as help them revise at night, or she'd do PE with her group, because she played volleyball very well and I think her pupils really liked her. I have always been of the opinion that there should be a degree of distance between teachers and pupils, and that distance is created by respect, not by fear or age: respect for knowledge and responsibility. But I also think each teacher has his or her approach and if she felt all right always being with her pupils and results in class were good, who was I to object? Last year her three classes all passed chemistry, with an average of ninety per cent, and not everybody can manage that, I told myself: if they're the results she gets, then let her get on with it! That might sound like Machiavelli but it's not Machiavellian. I did talk to her one day about the over-familiarity, but she just said she felt better that way and we never brought it up again. It's a pity this has happened, and yesterday we had attendance problems in the afternoon because very many pupils went to the vigil and cemetery, but we decided to turn a blind eye to their absence . . . And as an individual? I'm not sure. I didn't know that side of her so well. She'd a boyfriend who'd come to pick her up on his motorbike, but that was last year, although at the vigil Mrs Dagmar said she'd seen him waiting outside for her for three days. You know, Dagmar can tell you about her, she was her head of department and I think her best friend at Pre-Uni, but she's not in today as she's been really hit by what happened to Lissette . . . Yes, that's true, she dressed very well, but I'd understood her stepfather and mother frequently go abroad and it is quite natural they'd bring her a few things back, isn't it? Just remember she was also very young, this same generation . . . What a great pity, and she being so pretty . . ."

The bell brought an end to his oration: the previous gentle hum turned into the raucous shouting of an overflowing stadium and, youths rushed down corridors in search of the cafeteria, their boy or girlfriends and the lavatories where they'd inevitably indulge in a spot of clandestine smoking. While Manolo jotted down some details from the murdered woman's work-record, and the address of the teacher by the name of Dagmar, Conde went out into the playground longing to smoke a cigarette and inhale the ambience from his memories. He found the corridors packed with white and mustard coloured uniforms, and smiled liked someone cursed. He was going to kill a friendly ghost, by lighting up right there, in the most forbidden place, in the middle of the playground, on the compass of winds that marked the heart of the school. But he held back at the last moment. Downstairs or up on the first floor? He hesitated for a moment about where to do it. I preferred upstairs, he concluded, and went up to the male lavatories on the top floor. The smoke escaping through the door was like a signal from the Sioux: he could read "here we smoke pipe of peace" in the air. He entered and caused an inevitable stir among the clandestine smokers; cigarettes disappeared and everyone suddenly had an urgent need to pee. The Count quickly raised his arms and said: "Hey, I'm not a teacher. I've come for a smoke too," and tried to look relaxed as he finally lit up, the focus of the youths' suspicious gazes. To compensate those who'd been cut short by his appearance he passed round his packet of cigarettes, although only three took up his offer. The Count kept staring at them, as if wanting to see himself and his friends in those students and once again he thought there'd been a change: either they'd been very small or these fellows were very big; they'd been smooth-cheeked and innocent and this lot had full grown beards, adult muscles and over-confident stares. Perhaps it was true that they were only interested in getting laid; so what? It was their prime time. At the age of fifteen had *they* ever worried much about anything else? Perhaps they hadn't, for in those same lavatories, above the first sink, a famous piece of graffiti had captured the irrepressible desire of a sixteen-year-old: I WANT

TO DIE DOING IT: DOING IT, EVEN UP AN ARSE. That legend had declared its basic erotic philosophy, now covered by paint, alongside generations of more intellectual graffiti like the one the Count now read: DO COCKS HAVE IDEOLOGIES? He decided to put a question to them when he'd put his packet of cigarettes away: "Were any of you Lissette's pupils?"

Suspicion returned to the faces of the smokers who'd stayed in the lavatories, momentarily placated by the offer of a ciggie. They stared at the Count as he knew they would, and some of them exchanged glances, as if to say, "Watch out, this guy's got to be police."

"Yes, I'm a policeman. I've been ordered to investigate the teacher's death."

"I was," spoke up a pale, skinny youth, one of the few who'd kept smoking when the Count violated the collective privacy of the lavatories. He took a drag on his minimal fag end before taking a step towards the policeman.

"This year?"

"No, last year."

"And what was she like? As a teacher, I mean."

"And if I say not much good, what will happen?" probed the student and the Count thought he'd met up with Skinny Carlos's *alter ego*: far too suspicious and sarcastic for his age.

"Nothing whatsoever. I told you I'm not from the

51

Ministry of Education. I want to find out what happened to her. Whatever help you can give me . . ."

The skinny lad held out a hand to ask a friend for a cigarette.

"No, she was really nice-natured. She was good to us. She helped those who were in trouble."

"They say she was a friend to her pupils."

"Yeah, she wasn't like the old fogeys who're on a different wavelength."

"And what *was* her wavelength?"

Skinny looked at his smoking-den mates, expecting a helping hand that never came.

"I don't know. She went to parties, things like that. You get me?"

The Count nodded, as if he got him.

"What's your name by the way?"

The skinny fellow smiled and nodded. As if to say: I knew it . . .

"José Luis Ferrer."

"Thanks, José Luis," said the Count, shaking his hand. Then he looked at the group. "And please, if somebody knows anything that might help, tell the headmaster to ring me. If the teacher was really that nice, I think she deserves that much. See you," and he went out into the passage, after crushing his cigarette in the sink and reflecting for a second on the ideological conundrum etched on the wall.

Manolo and the headmaster were waiting in the playground.

"I was a pupil here, you know," he announced, without looking at their host.

"You don't say. And you've not been back for some time?"

The Count nodded and paused before answering.

"Quite a number of years, in fact . . . I spent two years in that classroom," and he pointed to the corner of the second floor, on the same wing as the lavatories he'd just visited. "I don't know if we were very different to the boys you have now, but we hated our headmaster."

"Headmasters do change from time to time," he replied, slipping his hands into the pockets of his *guayabera*. He seemed about to launch into another harangue, to demonstrate his insights and skilled control of that performance space. The Count looked at him for a moment, to see if such a change were possible. Possibly, but he'd take some convincing.

"If only. They sacked ours for fraud."

"Yes, we all know about him."

"But what nobody said was that several teachers were implicated. They threw out the headmaster and two heads of department, who were apparently the ones most involved in the affair. Perhaps the odd one of those teachers is still festering here."

"You trying to alarm me?"

"I'm just telling you the truth, maybe because that headmaster got rid of the best teacher we had, one who taught Spanish and did things the way Lissette did. She preferred to be with us and taught lots of people to read . . . Have you read *Hopscotch*? She thought it was the best book ever and said so in such a way that for many years I believed her. But I don't know if these youths are very different. Do they still smoke in the lavatories and play truant over the wall in the PE yard?"

The headmaster tried to smile and took a few steps towards the middle of the playground.

"Did you truant?"

"Ask Julián the guard-dog, the caretaker on the door. He probably still remembers me."

Manolo padded stealthily over, and stood next to his boss, but a long way from the conversation. Conde knew he must be eying up the girls, enjoying the scent of so many maidenheads under threat or freshly sacrificed, and then imitated him, but only for a few seconds, because he immediately felt old, terribly remote from those young blossoming girls, their yellow smocks cut to their thighs, cool as he would never be again.

"Well, I do apologize, but the fact is I . . ."

"Don't worry, headmaster," replied the Count, smiling at him for the first time. "We must be off. But I'd like to ask you a question . . . a difficult one, as you might

54

say. Have you heard any rumours about your youngsters smoking marijuana?"

The headmaster's smiling face, which had expected another kind of difficult question, turned into a caricature of a bad frown. The Count nodded: yes, you heard me aright.

"Hey, why do you ask?"

"No reason in particular, just to find out whether they are really that different."

The man thought for a moment before answering. He seemed at a loss, but the Count knew he was searching for the most politically tactful response.

"I really don't think so. At least I don't believe it to be the case, though anything can happen at a party in their barrios, I don't know if the drop-outs smoke . . . But I don't think so. They maybe couldn't care less and are rather frivolous, but I wouldn't say they were evil, you know."

"Nor would I," said the Count shaking the headmaster's hand.

They walked towards the exit where several students were trying to persuade Julián the caretaker to let them out on a really urgent errand. No, don't go spinning tall stories. If you don't have a headmaster's note then nobody's leaving, Julián was surely telling them, repeating the spiel he'd been rehearsing the past thirty years. So, they're not so different, it's the same old game, thought the Count, who, as he walked past the caretaker, looked him in the eye again, and while the man was opening the gate to let them out, he said: "Julián, it's me the Count, the one who used to get out over the back to go and hear the episodes of Guaytabó," and he happily left the past to return to the gusts in the present blowing away the last spring blossom from the *majaguas*. Only then did he notice that they'd cut down the two trees nearest to the steps, beneath which he'd won a couple of girls to his love. Sad, isn't it?

"I'm sorry, but I'm not free till about seven," and the Count thought that recently everyone was saying they were sorry and that the woman's voice was still as charming and confident as when she'd stated publicly that long hair down to the jaw best suited an angular face. "I'm finishing an article I have to give in tomorrow. Is that time all right?"

"Of course it is. We'll be there. Goodbye," he answered, checking his watch and seeing it was barely three-thirty. He hung up and walked back to the car, as Manolo started the engine.

"Well, what did she say?" he asked sticking his head out of his window.

"Not till seven."

"Blast her," responded Manolo hitting the steering wheel with both hands. He'd already told the Count he'd be going out tonight with Adriana his current girlfriend, a mulatto with the firmest butt you ever did touch, tits that got you horny and a face to . . . you know what. Look what she's done to me, he'd said, opening his arms, blaming his latest sexual conquest for the irretrievable deterioration in his physique.

"Come on, drop me home and pick me up at six-thirty," suggested Lieutenant Mario Conde, thinking he was not prepared to bus it to Casino Deportivo because Manolo had a desperate need to finger Adriana's backside.

The car drove off down the black slope of Red Square towards the grimy 10 October Highway.

"Call your lady-love and tell her you'll see her at nine. Caridad will be a quicky," suggested Conde attempting to relieve his colleague's frustrations.

"I don't have any option, do I? Why don't we go to see that Dagmar woman?"

Conde looked at the notebook where Manolo had jotted down the teacher's address.

"I'd rather not do anything until we've spoken to the girl's mother. Why don't you ring Dagmar and see her tomorrow? I need you to look into something else. Go to headquarters and have a word with the Drugs people. Try to speak to Captain Cicerón. I need them to tell me all they know about marijuana in this area and to analyse what turned up in Lissette's lavatory. There are several very strange things about this case and I'm most interested in the remnants of marijuana in the lavatory. It was really real amateurish to leave something behind like that."

Manolo waited for the lights to change on Acosta and then said: "They didn't steal anything either."

"Yes, if only a couple of things had gone missing, we could think that was the motive."

"Hey, Conde, are we really going to finish early?"

The lieutenant smiled.

"You're worse than a bedbug with insomnia."

"Conde, your problem is you've never seen Adriana."

"Fuck, Manolo, if it's not Adriana, it's her sister, you're always at it."

"No, my friend, this time, it's special. Just imagine if I'm thinking of getting married. You don't believe me? I swear by my mother . . ."

The Count smiled because he couldn't for the life of him recall how often Manolo had made the same pledge. It was astonishing that his mother was still among the living after he'd invoked her so often. He looked out at the Highway, packed with people desperately trying to catch a bus to return home to lives that rarely managed to be normal. After so many years working in the police he'd got used to seeing people as potential suspects whose wretched existences he'd have to scavenge, like a carrion crow, only to uncover tons of heaving hatred, fear, envy and frustration. None of the people he got to know on any investigation was ever happy, and that absence of happiness, now also impacting on his own life, seemed a sentence that was too long and wearisome for him to bear, and the idea of leaving his job began to shape into a firm decision. After all, he thought, what a joke: me putting order into other people's lives, how about setting my own right?

"Do you really like being a policeman, Manolo?" he asked, almost without thinking.

"I think I do, Conde. Besides, it's all I know."

"But if you like it, you must be mad. Like me."

"I like a bit of madness," Manolo confessed crossing the railway line without slowing down. "Just like that headmaster."

"What did you make of that guy?"

"I don't know, Conde, I don't think I like him, but don't take any notice of me. It's only an impression."

"As impressions go, mine's no different."

"Hey, Conde, I'll tell Adriana eight-thirty, right?"

"That's what I said, Manolo. Hey, you're a man who says he's had lots of women, did one ever play the saxophone?"

Manolo slowed down imperceptibly, looked at his boss and smiled: "With her mouth?"

"Go screw yourself!" yelped the Count, also smiling. There's no respect these days, he told himself, as he lit a cigarette a couple of blocks from home. He felt better now: he'd be free for almost three hours and would sit down and write. Write whatever. Just write.

I insisted on the Beatles. It may be your cassette recorder and you can kick up a fuss, but I want to hear the bloody Beatles, *Strawberry Fields* is the best song in the history of the world, I defended my tastes, adamantly, and why the fuck did you ring? He said, Dulcita. He was so skinny at times it seemed he wouldn't be able to speak and his Adam's apple moved, as if he were swallowing. OK, and what else? Dulcita's off. She's off, he said and suddenly I couldn't decide where the hell she was off to: home, school, the moon, to the Donkey's Back, when I realized I was the only donkey there; off means you're leaving; skedaddling, making a quick, swift exit, going off, with one possible destination: Miami. Going off means not coming back. But why? She rang me last night to tell me. I've practically not seen her since I had that row with her. She sometimes rings me, or I ring her – we're still good mates in spite of the way I shat on her with Marián – to tell me: I'm off.

The evening light shone through the window and painted the room golden. *Strawberry Fields* was now a sad song and we looked at each other without saying a word. What was there to say? Dulcita was the best in our gang, the defender of the meek and needy, we'd say to rile her, the only one who listened to everybody

60

else and the one we all loved because she knew what love was: she was one of us, and suddenly she was off. Maybe we'd never see her again to be able to say, Fuck, how beautiful Dulcita is, never be able to write to her, talk to her or even remember her, because she's off and anyone who's off is sentenced to lose everything, even the space they occupy in the memories of friends. But why? I don't know, he said, I didn't ask: that's beside the point, the point is that she is going, he said and stood up in front of the window and the bright light made it impossible for me to see his face as he said, Shit, shit, shit, she's leaving, and I realized he might cry on cue and would be right to, because even our memories would be incomplete, and he said: I'll see her tonight. Me too, I told him. But we never did: Dulcita's mother told us, She's ill, she's asleep, but we knew she wasn't asleep or ill. The fact is she's off, I thought, and it was a long time before I understood why: Dulcita, the perfect, the best, the woman who so often showed she was a man, a man ready for anything. We walked back, silent and sorrowful, and after we'd crossed the Highway I remember Skinny had said: Look, what a beautiful moon.

Conde had always thought he liked that barrio: the Casino Deportivo had been built in the fifties for a bourgeoisie that couldn't afford mansions with swimming pools, but was ready to pay for the luxury of a bedroom for each child, a nice entrance and a garage for the car they would surely have. The passage of time and the dispersal of most of the original inhabitants hadn't overly changed the area's appearance. Because it's a development and not a barrio, the Count corrected himself, as the car proceeded along Seventh Avenue while he looked for the intersection with Acosta, noting how quietly darkness fell there, without abrupt changes or strong winds, as if the contingencies and disruptions visited on the city were banned in that pasteurized reserve almost wholly inhabited by the new leaders of the new epoch. Houses were still painted and gardens tidy while Ladas, Moskovichs and newly acquired Polish Fiats, with their protectively tinted glass, filled the car porches. Few people walked the streets, and those who did walked with the peace of mind that absence of danger brings: there are no thieves, and the young women are all beautiful, almost vestal, like their houses and gardens; nobody owns mongrels and the drains don't spew shit and other offensive waste. It was here that Conde had been to some of the best parties of his time at Pre-Uni: there was always a combo, the Gnomes, the Kents, the Highlights and they always danced rock and roll, never ballroom or anything Latin, and the parties didn't end in bottle fights, as in his down-st-hell, trouble-making barrio. Yes, this was a place to live the good life, he told himself, when he saw the two-storey house – which was also beautiful, freshly painted with a well-trimmed little garden – where Caridad Delgado lived.

Lissette's mother's hair was blonde, almost strawberry, although traces of colour endured close to the skull: a dark brown she perhaps considered too vulgar. The Count wanted to touch it: he'd read that, when Marilyn Monroe died, after so many years of relentless bleaching to create the perfect, immortal blonde, her hair was a sheaf of sun-dried straw. Nevertheless, Caridad Delgado's still had a bright resistant sheen. Unlike her face: despite the advice she showered on other women, and followed fanatically herself, she couldn't hide the fact she was fifty; the skin on her cheeks had begun to furrow around her eyes and the folds shelving down the nape of her neck formed an unsightly bundle of flab. But she must have been beautiful once, although she was much smaller than she seemed on television. To prove to the world and herself that she retained some of her old glory and that "beauty and happiness are possible" she wore no bra under a jersey – through which her plump nipples poked threateningly, as big as baby's dummies.

Manolo and the Count entered the living room and, as usual, the lieutenant began his inventory of goods.

"Please sit down for a moment, I'll get you your coffee, it must have percolated by now."

A sound system with two gleaming speakers and a gyrating tower to store cassettes and CDs; a colour television and Sony video-player; fan-lamps on each ceiling; two drawings signed by Servando Cabrera where you saw two torsos and rumps in combat (in one, triumphant penetration proceeded honourably face to face, while in the other it was reached *per angostam viam*); the wicker furniture, rustic chic, wasn't the common stock that came to the shops from distant Vietnam. The *tout ensemble* was most pleasant: ferns hanging from the ceiling, different styles of tile and a mini-bar on wheels – where a pained and envious Count spotted a bottle of Johnny Walker (Black Label) that was full to the hilt and a litre flagon of Flor de Caña (vintage) that seemed so huge as to be overflowing. Living like that anyone can be beautiful and even happy, he muttered, as Caridad came back into view with a tray and three rattling cups.

"I shouldn't drink coffee, I'm really stressed, but it's a vice I can't resist."

She gave the men their cups and sat down in one of the wicker armchairs. She tasted her coffee, with an aplomb that included raising her little finger to show off a shiny platinum ring mounted with black coral. She took several sips and whispered: "The trouble is I had to write my Sunday article today. Regular columns are like that, they enslave one so; one has to write, whether one wants to or not."

"Absolutely," replied the Count.

"All right, how can I help," she countered, putting her cup down.

Manolo also leaned forward, put his cup back on the tray and stayed anchored to the edge of his chair, as if intending to get up at any moment.

"How long had Lissette been living by herself?" he started, and although Conde couldn't see his face from where he sat, he knew his eyes, staring into Caridad's, were starting to come together, as if pulled behind his nasal septum by a hidden magnet. It was the strangest case of intermittent squint-eyes Conde had ever encountered.

"From the moment she graduated from Pre-Uni. She always was very independent, I mean, she studied with a grant for years, and the flat was empty after her father married and moved to Miramar. Then, when she started university, she decided she wanted to go off to Santos Suárez."

"Was she worried about living by herself?"

"I just told you . . ."

"Sergeant."

". . . that she was very independent, sergeant, knew how to look after herself, and do I really have to go into all that now?"

"No, I'm sorry. Did she have a boyfriend?"

Caridad Delgado paused for a moment's thought and at the same time made herself more comfortable opposite Manolo.

"I think she did, but I can't tell you anything for sure on that front. She led her own independent life . . . I'm not sure, not long ago, she mentioned an older man."

"An older man?"

"I think that's what she said."

"But didn't she have a boyfriend who rode a motor-bike?"

"Yes, that was Pupy. But they broke up sometime ago. Lissette told me she'd rowed with him but never explained why. She never explained anything much to me. She'd always been like that."

"What else do you know about Pupy?"

"I'm not sure. I think he prefers bikes to women. You know what I mean. He kept on his bike the whole damned day long."

"Where does he live? What does he do?"

"He lives in the building next to the Los Angeles cinema. The Settlers Bank building. I don't know which floor," she said, thinking before she continued. "I don't think he had a proper job. He lived on repairing bikes and that kind of thing."

"What kind of relationship did you two enjoy?"

Caridad looked imploringly at Conde. The lieutenant lit a cigarette and sat back to listen. So sorry, my dear.

"Well, sergeant, not very close, you might say." She paused to contemplate the copper-coloured freckles dotting her hands. She knew she was on treacherous terrain and had to watch her every step. "I've always shouldered a lot of responsibilities at work as did my husband, and Lissette's father was hardly ever home even when we lived together and she was a student on a scholarship . . . I mean, we were never a very united family, although I always kept an eye on her, I bought her things, I brought her presents when I travelled, tried to please her. Relating to one's children is a very taxing business."

"Rather like one's weekly magazine column," interjected Conde. "Did Lissette talk to you about her problems?"

"What problems?" she asked, as if she'd heard some-one blaspheme, and finally press-ganging her lips into a smile, she lifted a hand up to her chest and splayed out her fingers before launching into a convincing list. "She had it all: a house, a career, was well integrated, was the perennially good student, had clothes, youth . . ."

She didn't have enough fingers on one hand to enu-merate so many blessings and possessions and two tears ran down Caridad's wan face. As she concluded, her voice lost its sparkle and self-assurance. She doesn't know how to cry, Conde told himself, and he felt sorry for that woman who had lost her daughter such a long time ago. The lieutenant looked at Manolo signalling him to halt the conversation there. He stubbed his cigarette out in the large, coloured glass ashtray and leaned back.

"Caridad, you must understand. We need to know what happened and we have to have this conversation."

"Yes, I know," she replied, flattening the wrinkles around her eyes with the back of her hand.

"What happened to Lissette wasn't at all straight-forward. They didn't do it to steal, because as you know nothing seems to be missing from her flat, and it wasn't simple rape, because they beat her up as well. And most alarming of all: there was music and dancing that night at her place and they smoked marijuana in her flat."

Caridad opened her eyes and then slowly dropped her eyelids. Something deeply instinctual led her to lift a hand up to her chest, as if trying to shield her breasts that shook beneath her jersey. She looked downcast and ten years older.

"Did Lissette take drugs?" the Count followed on deter-mined to force through his advantage.

"No, she didn't, how can you think such a thing?" the woman retorted, recovering some of her battered con-fidence. "That's impossible. She may have had several boyfriends or been a great partygoer or got drunk oc-casionally but she never took drugs. What have people been saying about her? Don't you know she's been a comrade from the age of sixteen, and that she was always a model student? She was even a delegate to the Moscow Festival and a revolutionary from primary . . . You must know all that?"

"Yes we do, Caridad, but we also know the night she was killed there was marijuana smoked in her place and lots of alcohol consumed. Perhaps they took drugs and popped pills . . . That's why we're so keen to know who might have been at her party."

"For God's sake," she then swore, anticipating the final fallout: a hoarse sobbing rose up from her chest, her face cracked and even her strawberry blonde resistant hair seemed like an ill-fitting wig. The poet was right, thought the Count, a man too addicted to poetic truths: that blonde was suddenly as lonely as an astronaut in the darkness of outer space.

"Do you like this area, Manolo?"

The sergeant thought for a second.

"It's beautiful, isn't it? I think anybody would like living here, but I don't know . . ."

"What don't you know?"

"Nothing really, Conde, but can you imagine a down-at-heel like me, who doesn't have a car, a pedigree dog or big money in a barrio like this? Just take a look, everybody's got a car and a beautiful house; I think that's why it's called Casino Deportivo: everybody here is in competition. I know the conversations off by heart: Dear neighbour and vice-minister, how often have you been abroad this year? This year? Six . . . And what about you, dear managing director? Oh, a mere eight times, but I didn't bring much back: four tyres for the car, a leather leash for my toy poodle, oh, and my microwave, that's just splendid for roasting meat . . . And who is more important, your husband who's a party leader or mine who works with foreigners? . . ."

I don't like this area much either," confessed the Count as he spat out of the car window.

Red Candito was born in a tenement on Milagros, in Santos Suárez, and still lived there thirty-eight years later. Things had improved in the tenement in recent times; the death of the next-door neighbour had freed up a room they'd gained without major legal complications – "because of my ballsy father" Candito had commented – to the only room in the family's original dwelling, and thanks to the high ceilings of that old *fin-de-siècle* building, devalued and turned into a rooming-house in the fifties, his father had built a wooden mezzanine reached by a ladder so it now began to seem like home: two bedrooms in the part closest to heaven, and the final fulfilment of the ancestral dream of owning their own bathroom, a kitchen and a dining room on the ground floor. Red Candito's parents were now dead, his elder brother was into the sixth year of his eight-year sentence for violent robbery and Red's wife had divorced him and taken their two children with her. Candito now enjoyed his extensive home with a placid, twenty-something mulatto who helped him in his work: the production of home-made women's shoes which were permanently in demand.

The Count and Red Candito had met when the Count started at La Víbora Pre-Uni and Candito was making his third attempt to pass an eleventh grade he'd never pass. Out of the blue, one day when they'd both had the door shut in their face because they'd arrived ten minutes late, the Count handed a cigarette to that coppery raisin-coloured youth and thus sparked off a friendship that had lasted sixteen years and which Conde had always made best use of: from the night when Candito's protection prevented people stealing his food during a school camp to the sporadic rendezvous of recent times when the Count needed advice or information.

When he saw him come in, Red Candito looked surprised. It was months since he'd had a visit and, although the Count was his friend, a visit from the police-man was never just a friendly occurrence for Candito – at least until the Count showed this one was any different.

"Well, fuck me, if it isn't the Count," he said after looking down the passageway and checking nobody was around, "what's brought you to this neck of the woods?"

The lieutenant shook his hand and smiled.

"Hey, pal, how come you always look so young?"

Candito stepped back and pointed out to him one of the wrought-iron armchairs.

"Alcohol preserves me on the inside and my head, that handy gift from God, on the outside: it's as hard as nails," and he shouted inside. "Put the coffee on, our pal the Count's here."

Candito raised his hands as if asking an umpire for more time, and went over to a small wooden cabinet and extracted his personal medicine for internal conservation: he showed the Count an almost full bottle of vintage rum that stirred up the thirst provoked by Caridad Delgado's impregnable bar. He put two glasses on the table and poured out the rum. Cuqui pulled to one side the curtain separating the living-room from the kitchen and smiled in at them.

"How's things, Conde?"

"Here I am, waiting on my coffee. Although it's not so urgent now," he replied, as he took the glass Candito was offering him. The girl smiled and silently popped her head back behind the curtain.

"Hey, that girl's a handful for you, isn't she?"

"That's why I get up to my tricks to bring in a few pesos," nodded Candito tapping his pocket.

"Until the day you get caught."

"Hey, guy, this is all legal. But if I get stuck in a corner I can send for you, can't I?"

The Count smiled and thought that, of course, he could. Ever since he'd started working as a professional detective, Red Candito had helped him to solve various problems and both knew the Count's helping hand in times of need was the other side of the coin. Apart from the one old debt and their years as friends, the Count muttered, as he downed a big gulp of luscious rum.

"This place is real quiet, isn't it?"

"They gave a house to the people in the front room and it's quieter than a morgue. Just listen to that silence, pal."

"Just as well."

"What's up then?" asked Candito leaning back in his chair.

The Count downed another big gulp of rum and lit a cigarette, because it was the usual scene: he never knew how to broach with Candito the fact he wanted him to act as his informer again. He knew that despite friendship, discretion and the business of doing an old friend a favour, his jobs went against the strict, street ethics of a guy like Red Candito, born and bred in that dicey tenement where macho values excluded from the onset any kind of collaboration with a policeman: with any sort of police. So he decided to put out a few feelers.

"Do you know a young lad by the name of Pupy, who lives in the Settlers Bank building and rides a motorbike?"

Candito looked in the direction of the kitchen curtain.

"I don't think so. You know, Conde, there's two worlds in this place, rich little boys and street kids, like me. And it's rich little boys who drive Ladas and ride motorbikes."

73

"But it's only three blocks away."

"I may know him by sight, but he don't ring any bells. And don't measure life in blocks: those people live the life of Riley while I have to try every trick in the book to get my wad. Don't put me in the shit. You know what the street's like. Anyway what's this fellow been up to?"

"Nothing so far. It's to do with a crime and a half I need to solve. An ugly crime. Murder," he said finishing his drink.

Candito poured out some more and the Count decided to get to the point: "Red, I need to know if there's a drug scene at Pre-Uni, marijuana, specifically, and who's supplying it."

"In *our* Pre-Uni?"

The Count nodded and lit up.

"And they've done someone in?"

"A teacher."

"Nasty . . . And what's the deal?"

"What I said . . . The night they killed her they smoked at least one joint in her house."

"But that's got nothing to do with Pre-Uni. I expect they got it somewhere else."

"Fucking hell, Red, who's the policeman here?"

"Easy, pal, take it easy. I'm just telling you: I don't reckon Pre-Uni has anything to do with this."

"The connection is she lives near here, about eight blocks away, and Pupy was her boyfriend, though it seems he was falling out of favour. I tell you: if someone's pushing dope in the barrio, it can get to kids at Pre-Uni."

Candito smiled and indicated he'd like another cigarette: his fingers were now crowned by long, sharp nails as befitted a cobbler.

"Conde, my Conde, you know every barrio has its pushers and it's not only dope that's in the air . . ."

"Naturally, my friend. Find out from people in the barrio if anyone at Pre-Uni is buying: a woman teacher, a pupil, a caretaker, whoever. And find out if Pupy smokes pot."

Candito lit his cigarette and took two drags. Then stared into the Count's eyes, stroked his moustache, and smiled.

"So pot hits Pre-Uni? . . .

"You know, Candito, that's another thing I wanted to ask you: was it around in our day?"

"At Pre-Uni? No. There were two or three hotheads snorting lines in those parties when the Gnomes or the Kents were playing, or people popped pills and knocked back rum – remember how those parties ended up? It was sometimes around, but one joint between a hundred. Blond Ernestico handled some in his barrio."

"Ernestico, you're kidding?" the Count reacted in a state of shock as he recalled Ernestico's mellow voice and tranquil demeanour: some said he was a shitbag;

others reckoned he was a shitbag times two. "OK, but that's past history. Now is what concerns me. You going to give me a hand?"

Candito looked at his sharp nails for a moment. He'll not say no, thought the Count.

"All right, all right, I'll see what I can dredge up . . . But you know the usual: no names, as the Yanks say."

The Count smiled sweetly wanting to take it a step further.

"Don't do that on me, pal, if they're pushing it to someone at Pre-Uni, there'll be one hell of a scandal, what with a murder thrown in."

Candito thought for a moment. The Count was afraid of a no-go he could almost understand.

"One day you'll get me burnt, guy, and no one will be there to drag me from the stake. By the time you get to me, you'll need to send the vultures packing," he replied, and the Count took a breath. He gulped another mouthful of rum and sought the best way to seal the deal.

"While we're about it, I've got a little number I'd like to lay . . . Are the shoes you're making any good these days?"

"Soft as peaches, pal, and a knock down at fifty little pesos for you. If you're broke, I'll give them away. What's size your chick wear?"

The Count smiled and shook his head.

"Fuck if I know what size she is, pal," he answered and shrugged his shoulders, and thought how he'd ask the next woman he met her shoe-size before he glanced at her bum or tits. You never know when the info might come in useful.

Mario Conde, like almost everybody, owed his most distant memory of love to his nursery school teacher, a pale-cheeked, long-fingered young woman, who sprayed him with her breath when she took his hands and placed his fingers on the piano keyboard, while a gentle feeling of disquiet stirred in a vague spot between his stomach and knees. From then on, asleep or awake, the Count started dreaming about his teacher, and one evening he confessed to Grandfather Rufino that he wanted to grow up so he could marry that woman – to which the old man replied: "Me too." Many years later, on the eve of his marriage, the Count discovered how that young woman about whom he'd never heard a word more after the summer holidays was back in the barrio. She'd arrived from New Jersey on a ten-day visit to her family and he decided to pay her a visit since, although he rarely recalled her now, he'd never been able to forget her entirely. And he was very pleased he did, because not even time, grey hair and flab had managed to erase the serene beauty of that teacher to whom he owed his first erection through touch, and a remote awareness of the necessity of love.

Something about that woman, that he'd anticipated rather than experienced as a mere five-year-old when Grandfather Rufino took him round the fighting cock pits of Havana, had re-surfaced in the figure of Karina. It was nothing precise, because apart from his school mistress's languid hands and unblemished skin, nothing else had survived in the policeman's memory: it was rather a mood of calm, like a blue veil, created by a miraculous sensuality that was at once restrained and irrepressible. He had no choice in the matter: he'd fallen in love with Karina as he had with that teacher and, when he spied on the house where the girl lived, he imagined he could hear the hot rhythms of the saxophone she was playing, as she sat on the window wall while night-time Lenten gales played havoc with her hair. Seated on the ground, he caressed her feet and his fingers ran over every joint, every hard or smooth place on the soles of her feet, so his hands might possess every step that woman had taken in the world before landing in his heart. Now does she wear a four-and-a-half or a five?

"That guy Pupy killed her, I bet you anything. He was jealous and that's why he killed her, but he fucked her first."

"Don't be ridiculous, nobody does that kind of thing these days. You know, savage, it was a lunatic that did it, one of those psychopaths who assaults, rapes and strangles. I saw the film last Saturday night."

"Gentlemen, gentlemen, have you ever stopped to think what would have happened if the girl rather than being a teacher had been, by way of example, you know, an opera singer, a very famous one, naturally, and that instead of killing her in her flat, they'd killed her in the middle of a performance of *Madame Butterfly*, in a packed theatre, at the moment . . ."

"Why don't the three of you go lick your arses?" the Count finally asked quite seriously, as his three friends smiled and Josefina smiled and nodded as if to say, they're only pulling your leg, my little Count. "The fact is they like playing the fool. I'll make the coffee and you lot can wash up," he concluded and got up to get the coffee pot.

Skinny Carlos, Rabbit and Andrés scrutinized him from a table strewn with what could have been leftovers from a nuclear castastrophe: plates, bowls, serving platters, glasses and bottles of rum bled to death by the voracious, alcoholic appetites of those four Horsemen of the Apocalypse. Josefina had thought of the idea of inviting Andrés tonight, who'd now become her general practitioner after a lot of new pain beset her three months ago, and, as usual, she'd anticipated the reasonable rather than random possibility that the Count, as starving as ever, would turn up – and then Rabbit also put in an appearance, he'd brought some books for Skinny, he said, and eagerly signed up for that priority activity, as he dubbed the repast well seasoned by the nostalgia of four Pre-Uni schoolmates now in the fast lane to forty. But Josefina wasn't daunted – she's invincible, thought the Count, when he saw her smile, after clasping her hands to her head for almost a minute, while the light of her culinary inspiration flashed: she could kill the hunger of that predatory foursome.

"*Ajiaco* sailor-style," she announced, putting her banquet stew-pot on the stove almost half filled with water, adding the head of glassy-eyed stone-bass, two of the sweetest, off-white corncobs, half a pound of yellow *malanga*, half of white, and a similar amount of yam and marrow, two green plantains and others drippingly over-ripe, a pound of yucca and sweet-potato. She squeezed in a lemon, and drowned a pound of white flesh from that fish the Count hadn't tasted for so long he thought it must be on the way to extinction, and, like someone keen to offload, she added another pound of prawns. "You could also add in lobster or crab," added Josefina, like a witch from Macbeth before the stew-pot of life, finally throwing onto all that solid matter a third of a cup of oil, an onion, two cloves of garlic, a big pepper, a cup of tomato puree, three, no better four small spoonfuls of salt – "The other day I read it's not as bad for you as they say, just as well" – and half a spoonful of pepper, almost completing that creation which had every

80

possible flavour, smell, colour and texture, with a last quarter of a spoonful of oregano and another such of cumin, cast in the pot almost in a mood of irritation. Josefina smiled as she started stirring her concoction. "There's enough for ten people, but with four men like you . . . My grandfather used to make this, he was a sailor from Galicia, and according to him this *ajiaco* is the daddy of all *ajiacos* and any day beats Castilian *pisto*, French *pot-pourri*, Italian *minestrone*, Chilean *cazuela*, Dominican *sancocho* and, naturally, Slav *borsch*, that hardly merits a place in this Latin stew competition. The secret lies in the mix of fish and vegetables, but you know, one ingredient is missing that you always add to fish: potatoes. You know why?"

Hypnotized by her magic incantation, gawping incredulously, the four friends shook their heads.

"Because the potato is hard-hearted and this lot is of more noble mind."

"Jose, where the hell do you get all this stuff?" asked the Count, on the edge of a nervous breakdown.

"Don't be such a policeman and take the dishes to the kitchen."

The Count, Andrés and the Rabbit voted to nominate it the world's best *ajiaco*, but Carlos, who'd downed three big spoonfuls while the others were still blowing the steam rising from their bowls, pointed out critically that his mother had often cooked it better.

They drank coffee, washed up and Josefina decided to go to see the Pedro Infante film they were showing in the "History of the Cinema" because she preferred that story of tip-top Mexican cowboys to the argument the diners launched into with the first round of the night's third bottle of rum.

"Hey, savage," said Skinny after downing another line of rum, "do you really think the marijuana has to do with Pre-Uni."

The Count lit his cigarette and imitated his friend's alcoholic style.

"I don't know, Skinny, I really don't, but it's my gut feeling. As soon as I stepped back into Pre-Uni I felt it was another world, another place, and I couldn't see it like it was our Pre-Uni. There's nothing stranger than going somewhere you thought you knew by heart and realizing it's not what you'd imagined. I do think we were more innocent and kids now are more crooked or cynical. We liked to wear our hair long and be transported by our music, but we were told so often we had a responsibility before history that we finally believed we did and we knew we had to shoulder it, right or wrong? There weren't the hippies or drop-outs there are now. This guy," and he pointed at Rabbit, "spent the whole day harping on about being a historian and read more books than the whole history department put together. And this fellow," it was now Andrés' turn, "decided he was going to be a doctor and he is a doctor, and spent every day playing baseball because he wanted to get in the National League. And didn't you spend your whole time chasing skirt and then get an average mark of 96?"

"Hey, Conde," Skinny waved his hands, like a coach trying to stop a runner dangerously on course to a suicidal out, "what you say is true, but it's also true there were no hippies, because they fumigated the lot . . . Every man jack."

"We weren't so different, Conde," then Andrés intervened, shaking his head when Skinny went to offer him the bottle. "Things were different, that's true, whether more romantic or less pragmatic, who knows, or maybe they treated us harder, but I think in the end life passes us all by. Them and us."

"Listen to him speak: 'less pragmatic things'," Rabbit laughed.

"Don't piss around, Andrés, what do you mean, passed us fucking by? You've done what you wanted to do and if you were never a baseball player, it was down to bad luck," countered Skinny, who remembered the day when Andrés sprained his ankle and was out of his best championship. It was a real defeat for the whole tribe: Andrés' injury put an end to all their hopes of having a pal in the dugout belonging to the Industriales, seated between Capiró and Marquetti.

"Don't think that for one minute. What the hell happened to you? You don't fool me, Carlos: you're fucked and they fucked you up. I can walk and I'm fucked as well: I never was a baseball player, I'm a bog-standard doctor in a bog-standard hospital, I married a woman who's also bog-standard who works in a shitty office where they fill in shitty papers that people clean themselves on in other shitty offices. I've two children who want to be doctors just like me, because their mother has put it into their heads that a doctor is 'somebody'. Don't try to pull the wool over my eyes, Skinny, or talk to me about life fulfilment, or any of that crap; I've never been able to do what I wanted, because there was always something more vital on the agenda, something someone said I ought to do and which I did: study, get married, be a good son and now a good father . . . And the mad things, mistakes and mess-ups you should make in life? Hey, and this isn't the bottle talking. Look at me . . . No, no wool-pulling please, even you lot said I was mad when I fell in love with Cristina, because she was ten years older than me and because she'd had ten or how ever many husbands and because she did crazy things and must be a whore and how could I do such a thing to Adela, from Pre-Uni and such a decent, good natured girl . . . You forgotten? Well, I haven't, and whenever I remember I think I was a big arsehole because I didn't jump on a bus and go after Cristina wherever she'd holed up. At least I'd have made one a hell of a mistake for once in my life."

"Too lucid by far," interjected the Count. "You're worse than me."

The Count, Skinny and Rabbit looked at Andrés as if the guy talking was somebody else: perfect, intelligent, well-balanced, successful, calm, confident Andrés, the Andrés they'd thought they'd always known and whom, clearly, they'd apparently never known at all.

"You're plastered," said Skinny, as if trying to protect Andrés' image and even his own.

"Something's badly wrong in the kingdom of Denmark," pronounced Rabbit downing another shot. The clattering of his glass against the table emphasized the silence that had fallen over the dining-room.

"Yes, it suits to say I'm drunk," smiled Andrés, asking for a re-fill. "Then we can all feel at peace thinking life's not as shitty as the songs of drunks would have us to believe."

"What songs?" piped up Skinny, trying to find a route to a more amenable conversation. Only the Count smiled, sourly.

"And today when I left Pre-Uni, I remembered Dulce. Do you remember the day she said she was off, Skinny?"

Carlos asked for more rum and looked at the Count.

"No, I don't," he whispered. "Come on, more rum, don't be so stingy."

"And have you never stopped to think what would have happened if Andrés hadn't done his leg in and had married Cristina, and if you, Conde, hadn't joined the police and had become a writer, and if you, Carlos, had finished university and become a civil engineer and had never gone to Angola, and had more than likely married Dulcita? Have you never stopped to think we can't turn the clock back, that what's done is done? Have you never stopped to think it's better not to think? Have you never stopped to think that at this fucking hour of the day we'll never buy another bottle of rum and that by now Cristina's breasts must have sagged? No, it's better not to think any more crap . . . Now give me what's left in that bottle. And bugger the mother of any of you who ever thinks again."

"No need to worry, they don't bite. And I don't start teaching until this afternoon," Dagmar said as she tried to smile at him, undecided whether she was embarrassed by her dogs' welcoming barks and bared teeth or was proud to be the owner of such diligent hounds. The Count found her in her doorway, defying the wind, waiting for him like a bride scouring the horizon for the boat that will bring back her beloved. The two ugly mongrels, eager to show their rapid reactions, soon subdued their ostentatious woofs and wagged their tails as they ended their wild act. She invited him in and pointed him to a sofa where the Count sank helplessly as into a bottomless swamp. He felt tiny and inferior under the high ceiling, even more remote now, in that airy, shadowy La Víbora house. "Yes, it's true, I got on well with Lissette the moment she started teaching at Pre-Uni and I think we were friends. At least I felt I was her friend and I was much upset by . . ."

Conde let her take a breath and was pleased he'd dispatched Manolo to talk to the forensic doctor. If the sergeant had been able to overcome his fear of dogs, he'd have launched a fresh attack right away. While he waited, Conde remembered again that it was Friday. Friday at last, he'd told himself when he opened his eyes that morning to discover miraculously that everything was in order and he didn't have a headache. Only ideas.

The moment his flabby descent seemingly came to an end and his policeman buttocks anchored to a spring that had survived the weight of a thousand bums, the Count smiled. She followed suit, as if apologizing for her welcome speech, and when she did she almost looked beautiful. Dagmar was around thirty but retained the fragility of an adolescent who has yet to blossom: big mouth and teeth as if in a growth spurt, eyebrows spreading to the bridge of her nose and a degree of imbalance between legs and arms that were over-long for her skinny thorax and tiny breasts.

"What can you tell me about Lissette's private life? Who did she use to go out with? Who was her current love?"

"You know, lieutenant, I don't know very much about any of that. I'm married and have a child and as soon as classes finish I rush back home. But she was, as you say, a modern girl, and not one with commitments like me. I did meet one boyfriend she had, Pupy, but they fell out, although he still went after her and picked her up from Pre-Uni every so often. He's a looker, for sure. I don't know what else . . . Come to think of it, she never said much about that side of her life."

"Had she been going out with a man who was in his forties?"

Dagmar's smile faded. She stroked her forehead with her long fingers, as if trying to chase away sudden pain or squash an unexpected train of thought.

"Who told you that?"

"Caridad Delgado, Lissette's mother. She mentioned him but didn't know who he was."

Dagmar smiled again and looked towards a distant corner of her house. In addition to physique which made Conde uncomfortable, the departmental head exuded an excessive sense of responsibility.

"No, lieutenant, I can tell you nothing about that man. She never mentioned him. I expect he was a flash in the pan."

"Perhaps, Dagmar . . . They say she had very good relationships with her pupils."

"That is certainly true," the teacher answered straight

away. She seemed pleased by the turn in the conversation. "She got on very well with them all and I think they were very fond of her. The fact is she was very young."

"Did she ever tell you why she didn't do her Social Service in the interior of the island?"

"No . . . Well, she did once say something about a step-father, I don't know if you are aware . . ."

"I imagined that must be it. When was the last time you saw Pupy around Pre-Uni?"

"On Monday. The day before . . ."

"Is there anything else you think it's important I should know about Lissette?"

She smiled again and crossed her legs.

"I don't know, just imagine . . . Lissette was like an earthquake; she turned everything upside down. She was always doing something, was always ready to have a go. And was ambitious: everyday she'd make it plain she could be much more than a mere chemistry teacher like me. But she wasn't one to climb over everyone else. It was just she was so full of energy. I can't imagine anyone wanting to do that to her. That was horrible, really barbaric."

A madman, a psychopath who beats his victims, then rapes and strangles them. Could Skinny be right? Or would everything be much simpler if she were an opera singer?

"Dagmar, there's something stands out in all this business and don't be afraid to answer me sincerely. I'll treat whatever you say confidentially . . . There was a party at Lissette's the night she was killed. Music, rum, and people smoking dope," the Count counted each element on his fingers and saw the surprise in the teacher's eyes provoked by the last item of information. "Do you have any idea if Lissette smoked? Have you heard any talk about dope at Pre-Uni?"

"Lieutenant," she said after pausing a long time to think. She passed her magician's fingers back across her brow, never once smiling.

"No, it's not very nice, I know," concluded the Count, "this is what you call serious."

"I can't imagine Lissette doing anything of the sort. I refuse to believe that. People can say what they like. It's not true people always speak well of the dead . . . And forget the idea about kids smoking dope in Pre-Uni. It's quite ridiculous. Forgive my plain speaking."

"You're forgiven," the Count conceded, struggling to lever his behind out of the quick sands of her sofa. When he'd recovered the two-leggedness that meant so much in man's evolution, he had to re-position his pistol that threatened to slip out of his waistband. He then thought perhaps Manolo should have been there, and in his honour, declared with suitable acerbity, "I'd had great expectations of this conversation. I still think you could have been more helpful. Remember someone is dead, a friend of yours, and any scrap of information is useful right now. Forgive my saying this, but I have a job to do: I don't really know why, but I think you're holding something back. Look, these are my contact numbers. If anything else comes to mind, ring me, Dagmar. I'd be very grateful. And don't be afraid."

He had legs of stone. He'd sit on a stool in the entrance to the cockpit, and, holding the rooster in one hand, lean his legs of stone slightly backwards so the back of the stool rested against the doorpost made of *caguairán*, the hardest of Cuban woods. He then stroked the cock, fingered its neck and breast, combed its tail, cleaned the sawdust from its feet and blew on its beak, and injected his own breath. He was always poking a toothpick in his mouth and I was afraid he would swallow it one day. He had some small scissors in his shirt pocket and when he'd caressed and soothed his rooster he'd say "Come on, you beauty. Up you get, you fine fellow." He'd take his scissors and start clipping its feathers, I don't know how he did all that with his two hands, moving the bird as if it were a toy and the cock moving with him, as the scissors trimmed and the feathers fell on his legs of stone and the cock became even more handsome, a perfect beauty, red thighs and red comb and spurs as long as needles, no, spurs of a fighting cock. By that time of day the sun was filtering through the branches of the tamarind tree and in that light Granddad seemed speckled by the sun, himself a huge fighting bird. The rich smell from the neighbouring bakery wafted on the air in the cockpit entrance, mingled with the unmistakable odour of feathers, the vapour from the liniment for the birds' muscles, the stench of fresh chicken shit and the aroma from the wood chips covering the floor of the enclosed arena. He will kill or be killed, he'd tell me, when he let the cock go to peck in the grass, sitting me on his legs, that felt as hard as stone. The fate of the cock was an everyday issue, and I wanted to tell him to give it to me as a present, that it was such a beautiful cock, that I wanted it for myself and didn't want it to be killed, ever. "Look at it scratch; look at it strut. This is a blue-blooded bird, it's got balls, can you see them?" and I thought a cock's balls never hang down, they're inside, and they drop them for just a second, when they mount the hen, but so quickly you never see them – until I discovered my Grandfather was a poet and that the cock's balls business was a metaphor, or a chance, happy association, as Lorca would say – a man who knew nothing about fighting cocks, but all there was to know about bulls and bullfighters, but that's another story: yes, you could see it had balls. I sometimes dream about Grandfather Rufino and his roosters and it's a dream of death: all those perfect animals died in some contest, and my grandfather died from a dearth of fights and poetry, when cock-fighting was banned and when he became so old his legs of stone went soft and he could no longer go to clandestine pits and be sure to run faster than the police. Then he aged to his bones: "Never start a fight if you're not intent on winning," he always told me, and, when he knew all was lost, he didn't fight any more. A poet of war. I don't know why I'm thinking so much of you today. Or perhaps I do: seeing him, his legs of stone and the stool leaning against the *caguairán* doorpost, I learned, quite unawares, that he and I shared the fate of the fighting cock.

"Go on then." Lieutenant Mario Conde looked out from the window of his third floor cubicle at the lonely crest of the laurel tree lashed by the wind. The sparrows that nested in its top branches had migrated and the tree's small leaves seemed about to perish after three days of non-stop buffeting: "Resist," he shouted to the leaves with a disproportionate, rival energy, as if the endurance of the leaves was also implicated in the struggle for his own life. He'd set up such ridiculous parallels, and always did so when something too intense was torturing him: guilt, shame, or love. Or a memory.

Waving a foot like a nervous ballet dancer about to stumble, Sergeant Manuel Palacios waited for the Count to turn round.

"What's wrong, Conde?"

"Nothing, don't worry. Off you go."

Manolo opened his battered notebook and began to improvise: "The only thing clear is that nothing is clear. The forensic says the girl had a high level of alcohol in her bloodstream, some 225 mill, and that given her physical make-up, she must have been pretty drunk when they killed her, because the abrasions show she didn't put up much of a defence. For example, her nails were clean, so she didn't scratch her attacker and she didn't have bruising on her forearms, as someone protecting herself would. He can't tell us anything about the marijuana. They scraped the flesh on her fingertips and did an analysis with reagents but nothing showed up. There's no analysis that can detect it in the sample, unless the sample comes from a smoker who's really hooked. Now for the juicy news: she had sexual contact with two men and there are no signs of violence in these contacts: no part of her sex indicates an unwanted penetration. The things one learns on the job, right? If entry is friendly, then it's all squeaky clean, as you say . . . The fact is there is semen from two men, one A-positive and the other from blood group O; that, as you know is much rarer, but the doctor swears on his mother that between one penetration – his words, Conde, don't look at me like that – that between one penetration and the next there was a gap of four or five hours, given the state the sperm were in when the autopsy was carried out. That means the first penetration took place before she was drunk, because the alcohol had spent less time in her bloodstream. You with me? And then he says, though he's no definite evidence, it seems the A-positive guy, the first in, is a man between thirty-five and forty-five, given the state of his sperm, and that the second, the group O guy, is more vigorous, say around the twenty mark, although some old-stagers have a youngsters' juice and that's why they can impregnate. All revealed thanks to a bastard sperm. And now for a shocker: you already in a state of shock? Well, Pupy, that is, Pedro Ordoñez Martell, the man on the motorbike, is blood group O. Not fallen off your chair yet?"

Without going to such extremes, Conde squirmed in his chair and leaned his elbows on his desk. His eyes settled level with the sergeant's, as if demanding his full attention.

"For once and for all, Manolo, are you or are you not squint-eyed?"

"You still fucking harping on about that?"

"So how did you find out about Pupy being an O?"

"Didn't you know I'm as swift as an arrow? One day they should award me the fastest policeman medal . . . I just thought I'd track him down as I wasn't going to see you for an hour, so I went to the Committee, asked after him, and from what they told me he's a semi-lumpen or a lumpen-and-a-half. He lives on buying and selling motorbikes. It seems his parents are upright enough and they're always rowing with him, but he couldn't care a damn. He's got a reputation as a charmer and fancies himself with the girls. I didn't try to see him or anything like that, but I had one of those brainwaves of which I have such a good supply and thought about the blood thing and went to see his doctor in case he had that bit of info and, of course, he did: "Oh, it's O, his doctor told me, and he confirmed Pupy is twenty-five. What do you reckon, Duke?"

"That I'm going to nominate you for the fastest policeman medal. But don't change my title, for fuck's sake," he protested meekly and went back to the window. It was a pristine midday: the light beat down equally on everything within reach and the shadows were severe and fleshless. At that moment a nun in habits ruffled by Lenten winds emerged from the church on the other side of the street. Original sin spares nobody, you know? Two dogs recognized each other, sniffed each other's rumps in a proper, orderly manner, in a gesture of good-will exploring a possible friendship. "So I take it two men, one around forty, and the other younger, were with her on the same night, but at different times and . . . probably neither killed her, right?"

"Why say that?"

"Because it's a possibility. Remember on that night of love, madness and death there was also a swinging party and . . . we need to speak to Pupy. And see if he knows who the forty-year-old is . . . Why don't you try to get us a drop of coffee?"

"So you're in the mood for thought?" asked Manolo as sarcastically as he could, and the Count thought better of asking. He watched the sergeant's fragile structure rearrange itself in order to stand up and exit the incubator, as they both dubbed that tiny cubby-hole they'd been allocated on the third floor.

As ever, he went back to the window. He'd decreed that that chunk of city, extending between the weeping figs that surrounded headquarters and the sea that was a faint, distant presence, was his favourite landscape. It encompassed a church without towers or belfry, various tranquil, painted buildings, clumps of trees and the orderly hubbub from a primary school. All that configured an aesthetic ideal under a sun that diffused outlines and melded colours following the rules of the Impressionists. It was true, he wanted to think: the Boss had asked him to sink up to his neck in that murky business where he'd barely found a toehold. He found it increasingly difficult to keep talking about death, drugs, alcohol, rape, semen, blood and penetration, when a redhead with a saxophone might be waiting for him towards the end of that very same Friday evening. The Count was still choked by the heartbreak from his last frustrated love, Tamara, a woman he'd desired over

97

almost twenty years, the one who'd been the subject of his most enthusiastic masturbations from adolescence to thirty-five-year-old maturity, only to discover, after a night of love they consumed and consummated, that any attempt to hold on to her had been a spurious fantasy, an adolescent mirage, from the day in 1972 when he fell in love with a face he'd registered as the world's prettiest. When will Karina get here from Matanzas? Is this woman on the cards?

He sank his finger into the bell, for a fifth time, convinced that the door wouldn't open, despite his silent prayers and despite kicking the ground: he wanted to speak to Pupy, to find out about Pupy and, if she were on the cards, blame him and forget the case. But the door didn't open.

"Where's the guy gone?"

"You know, Conde, people on motorbikes . . ."

"Well, I couldn't give a monkey's for motorbikes. Let's go to the garage."

They waited for the lift and Manolo pressed the B button. The doors opened onto a gloomy, half empty basement and a couple of American cars of indestructible 1950s vintage.

"Where's the guy gone?" the lieutenant repeated and this time Manolo thought better of responding. They climbed the ramp that led out into Lacret almost at the intersection with Juan Delgado. The Count now looked back up at the building from the pavement, the only one of its height and modernity in the area and then walked back to the Lada 1600 they'd driven from headquarters. Manolo put back the radio aerial he always removed as a preventive measure whenever he parked in the street, and the Count opened the right-side door.

"Fire away," said Manolo switching the engine on. The Count looked at his watch for a moment: it was just 2 p.m. and he felt the unpleasant sensation of having time on his hands.

"Turn into Juan Delgado and park on the corner of Milagros."

"Where we going now?"

"I'm going to see a friend," the Count mumbled when the car stopped a few blocks on. "Wait here. I've got to go by myself," he said getting out of the car and lighting up.

He walked down Milagros into the relentless wind and dust. His skin smarted again with the heat from that breeze sent from hell. He had to talk to Candito, had to rid himself of all commitments on that night he'd already staked out, and he had to have the info.

The passageway on the site was also deserted by that time in the early afternoon, so ideal for a nap, and he breathed with relief when he heard the tapping of a hammer from Red Candito's home-made mezzanine.

99

Hard at it. Cuqui asked "who's that?" from inside, and he smiled.

"The Count," he answered quietly, and waited for the young woman to open the door. Three or four minutes later, it was Candito who opened up. He was wiping his hands on a dirty rag and the Count realized he wasn't particularly welcome.

"Come in, Conde."

The lieutenant looked at Red before going inside, trying to imagine what his old pal from Pre-Uni was thinking.

"Sit down," said Candito, filling two glasses with milky alcohol from an unlabelled bottle.

"Gut-rot?" enquired the Count.

"It goes down a treat," replied Red and drank.

"If it's not too rough," conceded the Count.

"What do you mean 'rough'? This is a Don Felipón, the best gut-rot made in town. It costs fifteen pesos a time and you have to order it in advance. A limited edition, you know. You can't wait, don't tell me?"

"I can never wait. You know me."

"But I've to take it easy, pal. I'm risking my neck."

"Don't fuck around, Red, this isn't the Sicilian mafia."

"You believe that if you want. Where there's grass, there's brass, and where there's brass there are people who want to hang on to it. And it's boiling hot out there, Conde."

"So there is dope around?"

"Yes, but I don't know where it hails from or where it's heading."

"Don't try to fob me off, Red."

"Hey, you think I'm God the Father the all-knowing?"

"And more besides?"

Candito took another sip of spirits and looked at his old schoolmate.

"Conde, you're changing. Watch it, you're a nice guy, but you're turning cynical."

"Sod it, Red, what's got into you?"

"You mean, what's got into you, my friend? You're using me and you don't care a fuck. All you care about is sorting your problem . . ."

Conde looked into Candito's bloodshot eyes and felt disarmed. He felt like leaving but listened instead to his informer's spiel.

"Pupy's a young devil. He's into everything: he nicks bikes, sells the parts, buys greenbacks, deals with foreigners. He lives like a lord. Just look at his bike, a Kawasaki, a 350 I reckon, real sweet. What else would you like to know?"

The Count looked at his nails, pinkish, so different to Candito's long dark specimens.

"Grass as well?"

"Yes, you bet."

"He's got to be on file."

101

"That's down to you. You're the cop."

The Count finished his shot and lit up. He looked into Candito's eyes.

"What's got into you today?"

Candito tried to smile, but couldn't. He put his glass on the floor without taking another sip and started cleaning a nail.

"What do you think, Conde? What do you think's got into me? You know the street out there, you weren't born yesterday and you know what I'm doing doesn't go down well. It's no picnic. Why don't you let me get on making my shoes without all this dirt? I feel ashamed to be doing this, right? Do you know what it means to be a snitch? Come on, Conde, what's in it for me? You think I'm going to finger people and live a quiet life? . . ."

The Count stood up when Candito picked up his glass and finished his drink. He knew very well what was riling his friend and he knew that any attempt at self-defence would ring untrue. Yes, Candito was his informer: on the street, his snitch, nark or squealer. He looked at his friend, who'd defended him more than once and felt dirty, guilty and cynical as he'd just called him. But he had to have the info.

"I know you think I'm a bastard, you're probably right. You tell me. But I have a job to do, Candito. Thanks for the drink. Say hullo to your little raver. And remember that I want to give some sandals to a little piece I met," and he shook the calloused, gluey palm Red Candito offered up from the depths of his armchair.

The wind combed the main street in his barrio as if trawling for dirt and dust were its only mission in the world. The Count found it hostile and resolute, but decided to take it on. He asked Manolo to drop him on the corner by the cinema though he didn't tell him he only wanted to walk, to walk round his barrio on a day that didn't favour such exercise for legs and spirit, because the stress of waiting seemed as if it would be the end of him. Sergeant Manuel Palacios had learned from almost two years of working and co-existing with the Count that there was no point asking questions when his boss asked him to do something unusual. Conde's reputation as a lunatic at headquarters wasn't mere gossip and Manolo had experienced it more than once. His mixture of pigheadedness and pessimism, of non-conformity and pugnacious intellect were components of a mind that was too strange and effective to be a policeman's. But the sergeant admired him, as he'd never admired anyone else, for he knew that working with the Count was at once a party and a privilege.

"See you, Conde," he said before making a U-turn in the middle of the main street.

The Count looked at his watch: it was almost four and Karina would never ring him before six. Will she call? He wondered as he walked into the wind, not even bothering to take a quick look at what was showing at the cinema it had taken ten years to refurbish. Although his body was desperate to be horizontal in bed, the speed at which ideas were spinning round his head would defeat any attempt to shorten his wait with the oblivion of sleep. Anyway that solitary stroll through the barrio was a pleasure the Count allowed himself from time to time: his grandparents, father, uncles and aunts and he himself had been born in that exact location and wandering down that high street – that had carpeted the ancient path along which came the best fruit from the groves in the south – was to go on a pilgrimage into himself, to boundaries that now belonged to memories he had acquired from his family elders. From the time the Count was born to that moment that route had changed more than in the previous two hundred years – when the first Canary Islanders founded a couple of villages beyond the barrio and began to trade in fruit and vegetables, later to be joined by a few dozen Chinese. A dust track and a few wood-and-tile houses on the outer limit gradually brought those remote ends of the earth to the hubbub of the capital and, in the era when the Count was born, the barrio was part of the city, and was filled with bars, liquor shops, a billiards club, ironmongers, chemists and a modern, efficient bus station, set up to make it possible for the barrio to participate in city life. Nights started to

104

become long, busy and lit up, with a poverty-stricken, laid-back cheerfulness the Conde could only remember. As he walked into the wind on his way home, letting the gusts sweep away these idle reflections, Conde felt once more the sentimental communion tying him to that dirty, badly painted street where many things that had featured in his ragbag memories had long disappeared: Albino's fry-up stall, next to the school where he studied for several years; the bakery, where he went every afternoon to buy large warm loaves; the Castillito bar and its juke-box voices that found drunks to sing along with; Porfirio's liquor shop; the bus-drivers' union; Chilo and Pedro's barbers' shop, destroyed by the only really fierce fire in the barrio's history; the dance hall, turned into a school, where one day in 1949 a couple of adolescents found mysterious emotional bliss after only just learning of each other's existence, becoming his parents a few years later; and the notable absence of the cockpit where his grandfather Rufino the Count forged his dreams of greatness, now a barren waste without a single trace of those big cages, the smell of feathers, the fighting arenas and even the prehistoric shapes of the tamarinds which he'd learned to climb under his grandfather's expert gaze. Despite his sadness at the gaps, and his nostalgia for what was gone for ever, that was the space where he'd grown up and learned the first laws of a twentieth-century jungle as raw in its dictates as the rules of a Stone Age tribe: he had learned the supreme code of masculinity that stipulated that men were men, something you had no need to trumpet, only to demonstrate whenever the opportunity arose. And as the Count had had to demonstrate several times in that barrio, he wasn't worried about having to do so once more. The image of Fabricio unleashed a rage he couldn't restrain that boomeranged round his memory. And I won't have any truck with him, he told himself, as he arrived home and tried yet again to cast out that troublesome image and think of a future full of hopes and possible loves.

A quarter to six and still no call. *Rufino*, his fighting fish, quickly circled the interminably spherical goldfish bowl and came to a halt very near the bottom. Fish and policeman looked at each other. What the hell you looking at, Rufino? Get swimming, fish – and as if to obey him, the fish resumed its eternal rondo. The Count had decided to divide the time into quarters of an hour and had already counted off five equal slices of time. At first he tried to read, looked on every shelf of his bookcase and gradually discarded every possibility that at other times he'd thought more or less tempting. It was true he could no longer resist Arturo Arango's novels, the guy wrote lots and lots, always about crazy types who wanted to go back to live in Manzanillo and reclaim innocence through a lost girlfriend; forget about López Sacha's short stories, far too wordy and *recherché* and longer than a life sentence; he'd sworn never to read Senel Paz again, so many yellow flowers, yellow shirts, if only he'd write something a bit more devilish one day . . . he might suggest to him, for example, that he write a tale about a party member and a queer; and Miguel Mejides, forget him, to think he'd once liked his books, the yokel writes so badly and so pretentiously à la Hemingway. So much for contemporary literature, he muttered, and decided to try again with a novel that he'd thought the best from what he'd recently read: *Horse Fever*. But he couldn't concentrate enough to enjoy the prose and barely got past the second page. Then he tried to put some order into his room: his house was like a storehouse of the forgotten and deferred and he swore he'd spend Sunday morning washing shirts, socks, underpants and even sheets. Washing sheets, what a horrible thought! And the quarters of an hour fell by the wayside, heavy, like clockwork. Telephone, for fuck's sake, I'll give you anything: just ring. But it didn't. He took it off the hook for the fifth time to check it was working, and returned the phone to its cradle when he had recourse to the most desperate of measures: he would bring to bear all his mental powers, which were there to serve some purpose. He placed the telephone on a chair and another opposite the telephone. Naked, he sat in the empty chair and after critically eyeing his moribund testicles hanging in the air – and spotting two grey hairs – he concentrated, started looking at the gadget and thought hard: You're going to ring now, you're going to ring right now, and I'm going to hear a woman's voice, a woman's voice, because you're going to ring now, and it's going to be a woman, the woman I want to hear because you're going to ring, now, and he jumped up, "Fuck", his heart beating like mad, when the phone really did ring loudly and the Count heard – also for real, salvation at last – the voice of the woman he wanted to hear.

"Sherlock Holmes, please. Professor Moriarty's daughter here."

The Count's ego was having a ball. He'd always been vain and arrogant and when he could show off his gifts, he did so mercilessly. He stood in the entrance to his house and greeted every passing acquaintance and prayed Karina would pick him up when he had the biggest audience. He'd watch her drive up, all casual, and walk slowly over . . . Hey, look at that lucky Count. Hell, a chick with a car and so on. He knew the points that item was worth in the ratchet of values upheld by people in the barrio and he wanted to exploit it to the max. A pity the surly wind had scattered the group on the street corner, who'd scurried into some safe haven to down their twilight, troublesome alcohol, and a pity that they're shutting the liquor store because nothing liquid had arrived to attract a queue. The afternoon was getting far too quiet for his liking. Besides, he'd put on his glad rags: pre-washed jeans he'd bought with Josefina's help and a checked shirt, soft as a caress, sleeves rolled up to the elbows, worn for the first time to honour that special night. And he smelled like a flower: Heno de Pravia, a present from Skinny on his last birthday. He could have kissed himself.

He finally saw her drive past his place, twenty minutes after they'd agreed, reach the corner and U-turn before stopping on his side of the pavement, with a back wind and prow pointing promisingly towards the dark heart of the city.

"Am I very late?" she asked kissing his cheek warmly.

"Not at all. Three hours and no more is fine for a woman."

"Got to the bottom of the mystery?" she smiled, starting the engine.

"Hey, it's not a joke. I really am a policeman."

"Yes, I know: a detective like Maigret."

"All right, if you must."

The small contraption jerked into motion, not quite ready for the off, then sped off down the half-empty street. The Count entrusted his fate to the god who'd blessed the greenback hanging in the window and thought of Manolo.

109

"So where are we headed then?"

She drove with one hand and with the other tidied away the unruly hair that kept falling over her eyes. Could she see the road? She'd made up immaculately and was wearing a loose-fitting dress: its mauve flowers on a green background and its precise cut aroused the Count's desires; down south, where her knees were parted, and up north low down the back and deep into a swooping neckline. She looked at him before replying and the Count thought he had on his hands a woman who was too much of a woman, one he would fall hopelessly in love with: a feeling in his chest, a judgement that brooked no appeal.

"Do you like Emiliano Salvador?"

"Enough to marry him?"

"Ah, so you like a joke too?"

"Dearie, I worked as a clowning policeman in the circus and people loved it when I interrogated the elephant."

"Seriously, if you like jazz, we can go to the Río Club. Emiliano Salvador's group's playing. I can always get a table."

"Anything for jazz," the Count agreed telling himself it was a good idea to start with instruments that improvised everything in a life some great master had taped so well there was little margin for variation.

He thought the city seemed quieter, more promising, even cleaner from inside that car although he doubted his impressions were anything but circumstantial. But so what: he felt happy and relaxed with that chauffeur, sure he wasn't going to die in any stupid traffic accident; Lissette, Pupy, Caridad Delgado's decline, Fabricio's loutishness and Candito's reproaches meant little as they moved relentlessly towards music in the night and, of this he was more than sure, towards love.

"So I have to believe you're a policeman. A real policeman, one who calls the shots and puts you in jail and fines you for bad parking. Tell me who you are and I'll start believing in you."

Once upon a time, a long time ago, there was a boy who wanted to be a writer. He lived peaceful and happy in a not very tranquil, or even beautiful dwelling, not far from here, and spent his time, like all happy boys, playing baseball in the street, hunting lizards and watching how his grandfather, whom he loved a lot, groomed his fighting cocks. But every day he dreamed of becoming a writer. First he decided to be like Dumas, the father, the real one, and to write something as fabulous as *The Count of Monte Cristo*, until he fell out forever with the infamous Dumas for writing a sequel to that promising book entitled *The Deadman's Hand*: it's a very petty act of revenge for all the happiness granted to Mercedes and Edmund Dantès. But the lad persisted and looked for other heroes who went by the name of Ernest Hemingway,

111

Carson McCullers, Julio Cortázar and J.D. Salinger, who writes such moving, squalid stories like the ones about Esmé or the tribulations of the Glass family. But the story of our lad is like the biography of all romantic heroes: life began to put hurdles before him to overcome, which didn't always come in the form of dragons, the lost Grail or changed identities. Some arrived wrapped round in deceit, others were hidden in the depths of incurable sorrow, others were like a garden of forking paths, and he was forced to take an unexpected path that led him away from beauty and imagination and threw him, pistol in belt, into the shadowy world of bad guys, and only bad guys, among whom he must live thinking he was the good guy charged with re-establishing the peace. But our youngster, who is no longer so young, kept dreaming that one day he would spring the trap set by destiny and return to the original garden, back to the path he'd always dreamed of . . . In the meantime, he kept leaving behind affections that die on him, loves that putrefy, and days, endless days, devoted to walking through the city's filthy sewers, like the heroes of *The Mysteries of Paris*. The lad is alone. To feel less alone he visits whenever he can a friend who lives in a cold, damp attic he can't leave, because he's been paralysed ever since the bad guys wounded him in a war. He was a great friend, you know? He was his best friend, a true knight who had been victorious in many a crusade and was only brought to heel by a treacherous wound, after being tied and gagged. So he goes to see his friend every night, and talks to him of his daily deeds, the wrongs he has to right, and tells him of his joys and his sorrows . . . Until one day he tells him he may have found his Dulcinea – from La Víbora, not from distant Toboso – and that he's dreaming once again of writing and, more than dreaming, he is writing, of happy memories and nights of anguish, only because the magic halo of love that his princess Dulcinea wrapped round him brings him back to his dreams, to the most alluring . . . And everything must end happily ever after: the youngster, who is no longer so young, goes out one day to listen to music with his Dulcinea and they cross the city that is lit up, full of smiling, pleasant people who greet them because they respect the happiness of others, and they dance the night away, until the bell rings twelve times, and he confesses that he loves her, that he dreams of her more than of literature or the horrors from the past, and she tells him she also loves him and they live happily together and have lots of children and he writes lots of books . . . Oh, that's if the evil genie doesn't interfere and on the stroke of twelve Dulcinea doesn't flee forever without even leaving a glass slipper behind. And then he'll wonder: what can her shoe size be? And here ends this extraordinary story.

113

* * *

"And how much is true in all that?"

"Every word."

She took advantage of the break the musicians took to ask him that, then stared into his eyes. He poured the rum out, adding ice and cola to her glass. The lights dimmed and silence brought relief that was almost unbearable. Every table in the club was full and the spotlights tinged in amber the cloud of smoke floating against the ceiling, searching for an impossible escape route. The Count contemplated those night birds assembled by alcohol and jazz, a style that was too strident and flamboyant for his own taste: from Duke Ellington to Louis Armstrong, from Ella Fitzgerald to Sarah Vaughan, his traditional bent had only very recently allowed him to bring into the fold – urged on by Skinny's enthusiasm – Chick Corea and Al Dimeola and a couple of pieces by Gonzalo Rubalcava Jr. But the subdued lighting and glints gave the place a palpable magic Conde appreciated: he liked nightlife, and in the Río Club you could still breathe a bohemian cellar atmosphere that existed nowhere else in town. He knew the deep soul of Havana was being transformed into something opaque and humourless, as alarming as any incurable disease, and he felt the nostalgia he'd nourished for a lost world he'd never known: the old dives by the beach ruled over by Chori

114

and his bongos, the bars in the port where a now nearly extinct fauna spent hours with a bottle of rum next to a jukebox singing passionately along to boleros by Benny, Vallejo and Vicentico Valdés, the dissipated cabarets that shut at dawn, when people couldn't stand another shot of rum or their headache. The Havana of the Sans Souci cabaret, the Vista Alegre café, the Market Place and cheap Chinese restaurants, a shameless city, at times tacky, always melancholy in the remote memories of times he'd never lived, that no longer existed – just like the idiosyncratic signatures Chori chalked up round the city no longer existed, erased by the rains and oblivion. He liked the fact he was in the Río Club for his momentous rendezvous with Karina and only regretted a black dinner-jacketed pianist wasn't playing *As time goes by*.

"You come here often?"

Karina tidied her hair as her eyes soaked up the atmosphere.

"Sometimes. It's the place rather than the music. I'm a woman of the night, you know?"

"What does that mean?"

"Just that: I like to live by night. Don't you? I should really have been a musician and not an engineer. I still don't understand why I'm an engineer and go to bed early almost every day. I like rum, smoke, jazz and living the life."

"Marijuana too?"

She smiled and looked him in the eye.

115

"You don't tell that to a policeman. Why do you ask?"

"I'm obsessed by marijuana. I'm on a case with a dead woman and marijuana."

"I'm afraid the story you told me is true."

"It scares me. Is a happy ending possible after all that? I think the youngster deserves one."

She sipped a little rum and decided to take one of his cigarettes. She lit up but didn't inhale. The maracas sound of a cocktail being expertly mixed came from behind the bar. The Count scented the distinct heat of a woman up for it, and wiped away imaginary beads of sweat from his forehead.

"Aren't you going rather fast?"

"Not quite the speed of light. But I can't stop . . ."

"A policeman," she said smiling, as if she found it hard to believe they existed. "Why a policeman?"

"Because the world also needs policemen."

"And are you happy you're one?"

Somebody held the entrance door open for a few minutes and the silvery light from the street flooded the shadowy club.

"Sometimes I am, sometimes I'm not. It depends how I settle up with my conscience."

"And have you investigated who I am?"

"I trust to my policeman's nose and the visible evidence: a woman."

"And what else?"

"Does there have to be anything else?" he asked sipping his rum. He looked at her because he never tired of looking at her and, very slowly slipped his hand under the damp table and took one of her hands.

"Mario, I don't think I am who you think I am."

"You sure? Why you don't tell me who you are so I know who I'm with?"

"I don't how to spin a story. Not even a life story. I'm . . . yes, OK, a woman. And why did you want to be a writer?"

"I don't know, one day I discovered that few things were as beautiful as telling stories which people then read and know I've written. I suppose out of vanity, right? Then, when I realized it was very difficult, that writing is something almost sacred and even painful, I thought I just had to be a writer because I myself had to be one, driven by myself, for my own sake, and perhaps for a woman and a couple of friends."

"And now?"

"I'm not sure. I know less by the day."

The silence ended. The instruments were still quiet on the small stage, but recorded music started to come from the sound room. A guitar and organ played by a young married couple still on good terms. The Count couldn't identify the voice or the tune, thought it sounded familiar.

"Who's this?"

George Benson and Jack McDuff. Or rather the other way round: Jack McDuff first. He was the one who taught Benson everything he ever got out of a guitar. It's Benson's first record, but still his best."

"And how come you know all this?"

"I like jazz. Just like you know about the life and miracles of the Glass Children's septet."

The Count then saw several couples taking to the dance floor. The Benson and McDuff music was clearly too strong a temptation and he felt he had enough rum in his veins to dare.

"Come on," he told her, already on his feet.

She smiled again and put order and harmony into her hair before getting up to give full rein to the flowery wings of her generous, loose-fitting dress. Music, dance and then the first of their kisses on a night made for kissing. The Count found Karina's saliva tasted of fresh mangoes, a flavour he'd not met in a woman for a long time.

"It's been years since I've felt like this," he confessed before kissing her again.

"You're a strange one, aren't you? You're gloomier than hell and I like that. You know, you seem to walk the world apologizing for the fact you're alive. I don't understand how you can be a policeman."

"I don't either. I think I'm too easy-going."

"I like that as well," she smiled, and he stroked her hair, trying to steal the softness he anticipated in more

118

intimate hair that remained hidden for the moment. She ran the edge of her fingertips along the back of the Count's neck, unleashing an uncontrollable frisson down his back. And they kissed, rubbing their lips together.

"By the way, what's your shoe size?"

"A five, why?"

"Because I can't fall in love with women who wear less than a four. It's against my regulations."

And he kissed her again and met a slow, warm tongue attacking him, violating the space in his mouth with devastating dedication. And the Count decided to ask to take up residence: he would become a citizen of the night.

On mornings like that, the phone ringing was always like an assault and battery: machine-gun fire penetrating the inner ear, ready to pulp the painful remains of grey matter still adrift between the walls of his skull. History repeated itself, always as tragedy, and the Count managed to stretch out an arm and pick up the cold, distant receiver.

"Fuck, Conde, about time, I was ringing you till two this morning but you'd vanished."

The Count breathed in and felt his headache was killing him. He didn't bother to swear to no avail that this would really be the last time.

"What's new, Manolo?"

"What's new? Didn't you want Pupy? Well, he slept at headquarters last night. What do you think I should offer him for breakfast?"

"What's the time?"

"Twenty past seven."

"Pick me up at eight. And while you're about it bring a spade."

"A spade."

"Yes, to dig me out," and he hung up.

Three analgesics, a shower, coffee, shower, more coffee and a single thought: how I like that woman. While the analgesics and the coffee worked their magic-potion effect, the Count was able to think again, and be pleased she'd asked him to hold off for the moment, because in the drunken emotional state that came upon him at the start of the second bottle he couldn't even have pulled his trousers down – as he'd discovered in the early hours when he woke up dying of thirst and found himself still fully dressed. And now when he looked at himself in the mirror he was glad she'd not seen him like that: bags under his eyes hanging down like grimy waterfalls and eyes belligerently orange. He even seemed balder than the day before and, although it didn't show, he was sure his liver was down to knee level.

"Take it very easy, Manolo, for once in your life," he begged his subordinate when he got in the car and wiped a layer of Chinese pomade over his forehead. "Tell me what happened."

"You tell me what happened: did you get run over by a train or was it an attack of malaria?"

"Much worse: I went dancing."

Sergeant Manuel Palacios understood his boss's sorry state and didn't go above eighty kilometres an hour as he recounted: "Well, the man turned up around 10 p.m. I was just about to go and leave Greco and Crespo on the corner of his block, when he drove up. He was on his bike and we went after him in the parking lot. We asked him who the bike belonged to and he tried to spin us a yarn. Then I decided to put him in to soak. I think he's probably softened up by now, don't you? Oh, and Captain Cicerón says you should call in on him. Also, although the marijuana in Lissette's house was waterlogged, it's stronger than normal and the laboratory doesn't think it's Cuban: they say more likely Nicaraguan or Mexican – a month ago they caught two fellows selling joints in Luyanó and apparently it's the same kind."

"And where did they get it?"

"There's the rub. They bought it from a guy in Vedado but although they told us a lot about the guy we can't track him down. They're probably giving cover to someone."

"So it's not Cuban . . ."

The Count adjusted his dark glasses and lit a cigarette.

121

They should erect a monument to the inventor of analgesics. FROM THE DRUNKS OF THE WORLD . . . should be at the start of the inscription. He'd take flowers. He'd be human again.

"Full name?"

"Pedro Ordóñez Martell."

"Age?"

"Twenty-five."

"Place of work"

"I don't have one."

"So what do you live on?"

"I'm a motorbike mechanic."

"Right, bikes . . . Go on then, tell the lieutenant the story about your Kawasaki . . ."

The Count moved away from the door and came and sat down opposite Pupy, inside the red-hot arc from the powerful spotlight. Manolo looked at his boss and then at the young man.

"What's the matter? Forgotten your story?" asked Manolo, leaning over and looking him in the eye.

"I bought it from a merchant sailor. He gave me a document that I gave you last night. The sailor stayed in Spain."

"Pedro, you're lying."

"Hey, sergeant, don't keep calling me a liar. It's really insulting."

122

"Oh really? So it wasn't insulting to assume the lieutenant and I are a couple of idiots?"

"I've not insulted you."

"All right, we'll accept what you say for the moment. What do you reckon if we accuse you of illegal sales? I've been told you sell things from the diplomatic shop and make loads of money?"

"You've got to prove it. I've not stolen or dealt in anything, or . . ."

"And what if we do a thorough search of your place?"

"Because of the bike business?"

"And if some little green bills turn up, and such like, what are you going to say then, that they grew on trees?"

Pupy looked at the Count as if to say "get this fellow off my back", and Conde thought he should give a helping hand. The young man was a late, transplanted version of a Hell's Angel: long hair, parted down the middle, cascading over the shoulders of a black leather jacket that was an insult to the climate. He even wore high boots with double zips, and biking jeans with reinforced buttock pads. Those eyes had seen too many films.

"If you'll allow me, sergeant, can I ask Pedro a question?"

"Of course, lieutenant," replied Manolo leaning on the back of the chair. The Count switched off the lamp but remained standing behind his desk. He waited for Pupy to stop rubbing his eyes.

123

"You like bikes a lot, don't you?"

"Yes, lieutenant, and the truth is I know the beasts like the back of my hand."

"Talking of things you know about . . . What do you know about Lissette Núñez Delgado?"

Pupy opened his eyes and looked frightened to death. The balanced geography of the accomplished charmer's face fragmented as if hit by an earthquake. His mouth initiated a protest that didn't materialize, and shook uncontrollably. Was he about to cry?

"Well, Pedro, what have you got to say for yourself?"

"What are you after? I swear, lieutenant, that's nothing to do with me. I know nothing about all that. I'll swear by whatever I don't . . ."

"Hold it, no need to swear just yet. When was the last time you saw her?"

"I'm not sure, Monday or Tuesday. I went to pick her up at Pre-Uni because she told me she wanted to buy some of those thick-soled trainers I had, that were a hundred per cent legal, and we went to my place and she tried them on and they fitted, and then we went to her place to get the money and then I left."

"How much did you charge her for the trainers?"

"Nothing at all."

"But weren't you selling them?"

Pupy looked enviously at the cigarette the Count had just lit.

"Do you want one?"

"I'd really appreciate that."

The Count handed him the packet and matchbox and waited for him to light up.

"Go on, tell us about the trainers."

"It's nothing really, lieutenant. She and I went out for a bit, as you know, and it's hard to sell something to an old girlfriend."

"So you gave them to her as a present, I suppose? You didn't do a swap?"

"A swap?"

"Did you have sex with her on that day?"

Pupy hesitated, thought about refusing to answer, a private matter and all that, but decided against.

"Yes."

"Was that why she took you home with her?"

Pupy sucked his cigarette avidly and the Count heard a very faint crackle of burnt grass. He swayed his head, denying an act he couldn't deny, and started smoking again before he said: "Look, lieutenant, I don't want to pay for something I didn't do. I don't know who killed Lissette, or what mess she'd got into, and although it's not a very nice thing to say, I'm going to say this because I don't intend to be the idiot picking up this particular tab: Lissette was a hot number, that's right, a hot number and I went with her, for a good time, nothing serious, because I knew she'd leave me high and dry any moment – like she did when

125

she got to know a Mexican who looked like a leaking pie, Mauricio by name, I think. But she was wild in bed. Really wild, and I liked bedding her, to be frank, and she was a cunning bitch and knew it and did me out of the trainers that way."

"And you say that was on Monday or Tuesday?"

"I think it was Monday when she finished early. You can check that."

"Lissette was killed on Tuesday. You didn't see her again?"

"I swear by my mother that I didn't, lieutenant."

"Where did Lissette fish her Mexican boyfriend out from? Mauricio, you said?"

"I'm not too sure, lieutenant. I think she met him in Coppelia or somewhere nearly. The guy was a tourist and she picked him up. But that happened some time ago."

"So who was her current boyfriend?"

"Lieutenant, that's anyone's guess. I hardly saw her, I've got another girl, a little cracker . . ."

"But she was going out with a forty-year-old, wasn't she?"

"Yeah, but that wasn't her boyfriend," and Pupy smiled at last. "He was just one of her regulars. I told you, she was a whore."

"Who was he, Pedro? Did you know him?"

"Of course I do, lieutenant, he was the headmaster at Pre-Uni. Didn't you know?"

* * *

"I've come for a coffee," declared the Count, and Fatman Contreras smiled from an armchair tried and tested by heavyweights.

"The Count, the Count, my friend the Count, so it's a coffee, is it?" he asked, and against all the odds he brought his enormous landlocked whale of an anatomy to its feet, while cheerfully holding out a hand maliciously intent on dislocating the Count's fingers. Was it his only ponderous trick? The lieutenant made the most of his masochism and let himself be tortured by Captain Jesús Contreras, head of the Department for Foreign Currency Investigation.

"Hell, Fatman, let go, will you?"

"Not seen you for some time, my friend."

"No, but I missed you a lot. I even wrote you a couple of letters. Didn't you get them? People are right when they say the post is shit."

"Pack it in, Conde, what are you after?"

"I told you, Fatman, a coffee. Apart from that I've brought you a little present wrapped in cellophane. So you know you're not the only bearer of presents around here."

Then Fatman laughed. It was a unique show on earth: his general flab, paunch, the obese tits of a transgressor of the three-hundred pound threshold, began to dance to his guffaws, as if flesh and pap were only loosely attached to a distant bone structure, and it might be possible to witness a full striptease that would uncover the hidden identity of a skeleton concealed under three hundred and twenty pounds of flesh and fat. Watching him laugh, the Count always thought about the strange, predestined relationship between the Fatman's surname and his figure: he was simply Contreras, a round, chubby, voluminous and dense contrarian.

"Hey, Conde, nobody has given me a present since I was seven. Shit, seven at the very most."

"But do you or don't you have any coffee?"

Contreras was going to set off his laughter again but restrained himself.

"I always have some for my friends. And it's still hot."

He rolled, rather than walked, towards his desk drawer and extracted a half-full glass of coffee.

"But don't drink it all, remember I've used up my ration."

The Count took a more than generous sip and an alarming look of despair spread over Fatman's critical face. It was the best coffee you could drink at headquarters, specially sent to Captain Contreras from Major Rangel's strategic reserves. Before returning the glass, the Count had another swallow.

"Hey, you, that's it. Look at that . . . Well then, what can I do for you?"

"No, I've got something for you. A three-and-a-half litre Kawasaki that came from who knows where, purchases from the diplo shop and an almost definite currency swindle. He's a real joy. I've got him in my office and he's so ripe he's about to fall from the tree. I'll make him a present to you on condition that you hold on to him for a while because I've not done with him yet. Like the idea?"

"I like it," replied Fatman Contreras, who could contain himself no longer: he let his laughter rip and the Count thought one day he'd bring the walls down.

"Go on, push, come in," thundered the voice when the Count put his hand on the door handle. The bastard can smell me, thought the lieutenant as he pushed on the door's frosted glass. Major Antonio Rangel swayed apathetically in his revolving chair and looked pleased, against all expectations. The Count sniffed: a delicate scent of fine, young but well-cured tobacco floated on the air. The Count glanced down: a long, olive-coloured cheroot was languishing on the ashtray.

"And what is that?"

"A Davidoff 5000, what did you think?"

"I'm happy for your sake."

"I am for yours." The major stopped swaying and picked up the cigar. He sucked on it as if it were ambrosia. "You see, I'm in a good . . . Where the hell did you get to? Or have you gone freelance? You do know I serve a purpose here?"

The Count sat down opposite the major and tried to smile.

Rangel demanded to know each step taken in each investigation by each subordinate, particularly if the subordinate happened to be Mario Conde. Although he had more confidence in the lieutenant's abilities than in his own, the major was afraid of him. He knew the Count's devious ways and tried to keep him on the shortest possible leash. The Count thought of a couple of jokes right away and decided he might as well try one out: "Major, I've come to ask for early retirement."

The Boss looked at him for a moment and, without flinching, returned his cigar to the ashtray.

"Ah, so that was it," he replied quietly with a yawn. "Go down to personnel and tell them to get the papers ready and I'll sign them. It will do my blood pressure good. I'll finally be able to work without the stress . . ."

The Count smiled, deflated.

"Fuck, Boss, can't even joke with you now."

"You never could!" the Boss bellowed. "I don't know how you dare. Hey, Count, I really would like to know why the hell you joined the force?"

"I only answer that kind of question in the presence of my lawyer."

"To hell with you, Roman law and the Society of Lawyers. How's the case going? It's Saturday already."

130

The Count lit his cigarette and looked at the clear sky through the office window. Would you never see clouds through that window?

"Slowly. We've just interrogated one of the suspects, Pupy, a wheeler-dealer who was the girl's boyfriend. For the moment I don't think he was involved in her death, he's got an alibi with too many witnesses, but he confirmed two things that give this rumba a new tune: the teacher was a hot number, as he put it, quicker at getting a Colt out than Billy the Kid, and she was having an affair with the head teacher at Pre-Uni, who's now the second suspect. But there's something odd in all this. The forensic says the girl's last sexual contact, just before she was killed, was with a young twenty-something, who belongs to the blood group O. And Pupy has this kind of blood . . . The head is in his forties and might be the person who had it off with her five or six hours earlier. But if it's true, as it seems likely, that Pupy didn't see her on Tuesday night because he was out with a motorbike gang in the Havana Club in Santa María, and wasn't the last to have it off with her, who was? And if Pupy didn't kill her, who did? The head's number is in this raffle, but one thing doesn't fit: the party that night, the drinking and the pot smoking. I'm not a fan of the headmaster but he doesn't seem one to be in the thick of that. Though they could have killed her after the party . . . What do you reckon, Boss?"

The major got out of his chair and set his Davidoff to work. That rich tobacco was a bowl of incense spreading its fragrance each time the Boss exhaled.

"Bring me the tape with Pupy, I want to listen to him. Why do you think it wasn't him? Have you checked his story?"

"I told Crespo and Greco to check it out, but I'm pretty sure. He gave me too many names to have made it up. Besides, I have this hunch it wasn't him . . ."

"Listen, I bristle with fear whenever you have a hunch. And why did you take against the head?"

"I don't know, perhaps because he's a head teacher. He acts as if he was born to be one; that's why."

"So that's what you don't like . . . And you say the girl was a bit crazy? The report . . ."

"It was an official report, Boss. You never hear it said that anything goes on paper? You can't imagine everything there might be behind that document: opportunism, hypocrisy, a desire to get up the greasy pole and much more besides. But that paper says she was an example for the youth . . ."

"Forget it, don't teach your granddaddy to suck eggs. I was doing this before you knew how to clean the snot . . . You know, Mario, I reckon you're slowing down. What's up?"

The Count stubbed out his cigarette in the ashtray before replying: "I don't know, Boss, there's something

I don't get in all this, you know, the marijuana factor – not knowing where it came from makes me like I can't concentrate."

The major's gesture was theatrical and perfect: he raised his hands to his head and looked towards the ceiling, as if looking for heaven's mercy.

"Now that is the straw that broke the camel's back. I'll let you retire right now. So it's all down to a problem of concentration, is it?"

"But I feel fine, Boss."

"With that shitty look on your face? . . . Mario, Mario, remember what I told you: keep it above board, whatever your impulses. Don't put one foot out of line, or I'll amputate it myself."

"But, Boss, what's it all about? What's the real story?"

"I told you I don't know, but I can smell something's brewing. There's an investigation around that comes from the very top. I don't know what's up or what they're looking for, but it's a big deal and heads will roll . . . And don't ask me any more questions . . . Hey, did you know I got a little parcel and letter from my daughter yesterday? Apparently it's all going well with her Austrian ecologist. They're living in Vienna, I did tell you that, didn't I?"

"I'd love to live in Vienna. I'd try my arm at leading the girls' choir. Twenty-year-old . . . Does Vienna have police?"

"In the letter she told me she'd been to Geneva with her husband, to one of those meetings about whales, and you know where she went: to Zino Davidoff's tobacconist shop. She says it's a beautiful place and bought me a box of five cigars . . . You can't imagine how much I miss her, Mario. I don't know why my little girl had to leave here."

"Because she fell in love, Boss, what more do you want? Look, I'm also in love and if I'm told we're going to New Orleans, I'll go with her."

"New Orleans? You're in love? What's this all about?"

"No, it's just to listen to blues, soul, jazz and the like."

"Off you go, Mario, I can't stand any more. You've got forty-eight hours to settle this one. If not, don't even bother coming for your pay at the end of the month."

The Count got up and looked at his boss. He dared again: "That's OK, love feeds . . ." he declared on his way to the door.

"You'll be starving soon enough . . . Hey, did you hear about Jorrín? He had a bad turn on Wednesday night. It was very peculiar: a pre-heart attack, they say. I went to see him yesterday and he asked after you. He's in the Clinic on Twenty-sixth. You know, Mario, I think that's it for Jorrín the policeman."

The Count thought about Captain Jorrín, the old sea-dog at headquarters. And remembered how he'd never met up with him outside the walls of that building in ten years. He was always promising to pay him a call, to sit down with him and have a coffee, a few shots of rum,

134

and talk about what people usually talk about – and in the end he never kept his promise. Were they friends? He felt unbelievably guilty when he told his chief: "How shitty, right?" and walked out leaving his chief wrapped in a cloud of blue, fragrant Davidoff 5000 smoke, a 14.2 centimetre Gran Corona, from the 1988 Vueltabajo crop, sold in Geneva by the tsar himself: Zino Davidoff.

There are people who are luckier and can trust to the fate God or the devil has planned for them. I'm not one, I'm a disaster, and worse still, I sometimes take a gamble, and you know, fuck everything up. What is going to happen now? Yes, it's true. I thought about giving you a ring and telling you, but shied off. I was scared: scared you might connect me with what happened, scared my wife might find out, scared they'd find out at Pre-Uni and lose their respect for me . . . I'm not ashamed to tell you: I'm afraid. But I wasn't involved in what happened. How could I ever do anything like that? I was mad about her and even thought of talking to my wife and telling her, but Lissette didn't want me to, she said it was too soon, she didn't want to go public, she was too young. A disaster. No, just two months ago. When we were at the school camp. You know it's different there, more relaxed than in school and it almost started like a game, she was still Pupy's girlfriend, the biker, and I thought it was no go, that it was just a dirty old man's wishful thinking – but when we returned to Havana, one day when we finished a meeting around seven, I asked her if she'd invite me for a coffee and that's how it began. But I'm sure nobody knew. Do you think I could ever harm her? I think Lissette was one of the best things to happen to me, she gave me a reason to live, to do crazy things, to abandon everything, even to forget my fate, because she might be my fate . . . Out of jealousy? What jealousy? She'd split up with Pupy, she swore it was all over, and when you're forty-six and a woman twenty years younger says that you just have to believe her or go home and sweep the backyard and devote yourself to chicken-breeding . . . I was going to see her earlier that day, but this job is hell, if it's not Juan, it's Pedro, and if it's not the Party it's the Town Hall, and I left here around six-thirty. I was at her place just over an hour, no longer, because when I got home the eight-thirty soap was beginning . . . Well, yes, we did have sexual relations, that's reasonable enough, isn't it? A positive? That's right, how did you find out? So, you know the whole lot, don't you? Yes, I spent that whole night at home. I had to prepare a report for the following day, that's why I left Pre-Uni so late that day. Yes, my wife was there and one of the children, the youngest, the other's sixteen and goes out almost every night, he's got a girlfriend now. Yes, my wife can confirm that, but please, is it really necessary? Don't you believe me? I know, it's your job,

136

but I'm a person, not a lead . . . What do you want, my world to collapse around me? Who do you want me to swear by? No, she wasn't going with anyone else, I do know that for a fact, they must have raped her, for she was raped, wasn't she? Didn't they rape and then kill her? Why do you force me to talk about all this, for fuck's sake? It's like being punished because I believed I could still feel I was alive, alive like her . . . I'm scared . . . Yes, he's a good student, has he done something? Just as well. Yes, the office will give you the address . . . But what's going to happen now? My wife? If I'd been lucky . . .

Hospitals are suffused with an odour of pain and sorrow: ether, anaesthetics, aerosols, alcohol you can't drink . . . The one test Conde wanted never to face again was being admitted to hospital. The months when he watched over Skinny's agonizing sleep, when he was skinnier than ever, on his front in bed, his back shattered, his legs useless and that colour of murky glass in his eyes, had given him memories for ever of the unique smell of suffering. Two operations in two months, all his hopes dashed in two months, his whole life changed in two months: a wheelchair and paralysis creeping like a slowly burning fuse, eating up nerves and muscles until one day it would reach his heart and burn him to death. Once again he recognized that hospital odour as he walked through

137

the foyer – empty at that time in the afternoon – and, without saying a word, he almost rubbed his police credentials in the eyes of the guard who came between them and the lift.

They looked for a signpost on the third-floor corridor. Room 3-48 must be on the left, according to the notice sergeant Manuel Palacios had seen, and they walked on counting off the even-numbered cubicles.

The Count looked in and saw Captain Jorrín's un-shaven face on the raised head of a Fowler bed. By his side, on the indispensable chair, a tired-looking woman in her fifties stopped swaying gently and stared at them questioningly. She got up and walked towards the corridor.

"Lieutenant Mario Conde and Sergeant Manuel Palacios," said the Count by way of introduction. "We're colleagues of the captain."

"Milagros, I'm Milagros, the wife of . . ."

"How is he?" asked Manolo, peering in again.

"He's better. He's sedated so he can sleep," and she glanced at her watch. "I'll wake him up. He's got his medicine at three."

The Count went to stop her, but she was already on her way to the sleeping form and whispering something while she stroked his forehead. Jorrín's eyes strained to open a fraction, his eyelids flickering as he attempted a smile.

"The Count," he said, and lifted an arm to shake the lieutenant's hand. "How are you, sergeant?" he also greeted Manolo.

"Maestro, how could you do this? I think they'll try you for insubordination and then shut down headquarters," smiled the Count and forced Captain Jorrín to respond.

"Conde, even good cars end up as scrap."

"But a new part will get them back on the road."

"Do you really think so?"

"Tell me how you feel."

"Strange. Very sleepy. I get nightmares . . . Do you realize this is the first time in my life I've dozed off after lunch?"

"It's true," said his wife, and she caressed his forehead again. "But I tell him he's got to look after himself now. Isn't that so, lieutenant?"

"Of course it is," agreed the Count knowing full well the cliché was absurd: he knew that Jorrín had no desire to look after himself, he wanted to get up, go back to headquarters, and get back on the street hunting out bastards, murderers, thieves, rapists, embezzlers – because that, and not sleeping at midday, was what he was about in life, and he did it well. Everything else was a more or less slow death, but death all the same.

"How's it going, Conde? Out with this lunatic again?"

"No alternative, maestro. I should leave him here and take you with me. Perhaps they'll operate on him and make a human . . ."

"I was surprised you hadn't called in."

"I only just found out. The Boss told me. I'm busy on a case."

"What are you up to?"

"Nothing out of this world. A petty theft."

"He can't speak for very long," his wife piped up, now holding one of his hands. You could see the mark left by the plaster and the needle from a saline solution. Jorrín in defeat. Unbelievable, the Count told himself.

"Don't worry, we'll be off now. When are they going to kick you out of here, maestro?"

"I don't know yet. In three or four days. I've got a case pending and I want to see . . ."

"Don't worry about that now. Someone will take it on. Not as well as you, but someone will. All right then, we'll come tomorrow. I'll probably want to ask you a thing or two."

"Get better, captain," said Manolo shaking his hand.

"Make sure you do, Conde."

"You bet, but look after yourself, maestro, not many of us good'uns left," replied the Count, holding the old timer's hand in his. Although he recognized a nicotine stain on the fingers that even darkened the nails, it wasn't the tough hand he was used to and that alarmed him. "Maestro, I realized today we'd never exchanged a word outside headquarters. What a disaster!"

140

"A police-style disaster, Conde. But you just have to accept them. Although you know there's no such thing as a happy policeman, that you're a guy nobody can trust and that sometimes even your own children are scared of you because of what you stand for, although your nerves go to pieces and you're impotent at the age of fifty . . ."

"What's that you're saying now?" his wife interjected, trying to keep him calm. "Get some rest, go on."

"A police-style disaster, maestro. See you around," said the Count letting go of the captain's hand. Now the hospital reeked of suffering and of death.

"Off to the Zoo," came the order from the Count as he got into the car, and Manolo didn't dare ask: do you want to see the monkeys? He knew that the Count was feeling low as he lifted his matador's cape to let him in. He switched on the engine and drove out on to Twenty-sixth Avenue and soon slowly drove the few blocks to the Zoo. "Park close to a shrub for shade."

They left behind the ducks, pelicans, bears and monkeys and Manolo stopped the car next to an ancient poplar tree. The southern wind was still blowing and whistling insistently through the foliage in the park.

"Jorrín's dying," the Count commented and lit a cigarette on the fag end he'd been smoking. He looked at his fingers and wondered why they weren't nicotine-stained.

141

"And you'll kill yourself if you go on smoking like that."

"Piss off, Manolo."

"On your head, pal."

The Count looked to his right at a group of kids watching the skinny, aging lions that preferred not to walk, worn out by the hot breeze. The air stank of old piss and new shit.

"I'm at a loss, Manolo, because I don't think Pupy or the head were involved in what happened on Tuesday night."

"Look, Conde, let me tell you . . ."

"Go on, tell me, that's why we've come here."

"Well, the head has a good alibi and it seems to stand up. It's his word and his wife's, if his wife is in agreement. And if Pupy didn't really sleep with Lissette the night she was killed, what are we left with? The party: rum, music and marijuana. That's where it's at, right?"

"Looks like it, but how are we going to unravel this particular skein? And what if Pupy lied to us? I don't think he needed to set up an alibi with so many people, but then there aren't many people with blood group O and the last person with her was that, group O."

"Do you want me to tighten the screws on him?"

The Count threw his cigarette out the window and shut his eyes. The image of a woman dancing in the shadows came to his mind. He shook his head, as if trying to frighten that happy, inappropriate shade away. He didn't want to mix up potential bliss with the sordid nature of work.

"Leave him with Contreras for a bit and then we'll squeeze him some more until the juice comes out . . . And let's check out the head's story down to the last second. He's going to find out what it is to be really scared . . ."

"Hey, Conde, what do you think about the Mexican tourist who was Lissette's boyfriend? Mauricio, right?"

"Yes, so Pupy said . . . And the marijuana is from Central America or Mexico. Can that Mexican have given it to her?"

"Conde, Conde," Manolo then got alarmed, and even rapped the steering-wheel. "And what if the Mexican came back?"

The lieutenant nodded. Manolo had his uses.

"Yes, that could be. We must speak to Immigration. Today. But meanwhile I'm going to have another go at unravelling the skein. Marijuana: I don't why, but I'm sure that's where we've got to go. All right, get this piece of junk moving. This zoo smells of ammonia. Anyway, I've always thought of zoos as being like a kick up the backside. Let's go and call the Head of Immigration – take the coastal road.

The sea, like the enigma of death or the excesses of destiny, always provoked an obsessive fascination in the mind of Mario Conde. That dark, unfathomable expanse of blue attracted him in a way that was at once morbid and pleasant, like a dangerous woman you prefer not to flee. Others before him had felt the same secretions from that irresistible seduction and that's why they'd responded to her siren call. Nothing in his intimate memory was at all related to the sea: he was born in a poverty-stricken, arid barrio buried deep in the city's hinterland. But perhaps his awareness as an islander, inherited from the distant insular origins of his great-grandfather Teodoro Altarriba, alias the Count, a Canary Island swindler who crossed an ocean searching for another island far from creditors and police, was prompted by the simple vista of water and waves, of the line of the horizon where his eyes now lingered, as if he wanted to see beyond that illusory border, apparently the final frontier for all hopes. The Count, sitting by the coast, thought again of the rare perfection of the world that divided its space up to make life richer and more complex yet, at the same time, separate men and even their thoughts. At one time in his life such ideas and fascination for the sea related to a desire to travel and explore and fly over other worlds from which the ocean separated him – Alaska and its explorers and sledges, Australia, Sandokan's Borneo – but he'd long since assumed his destiny as a man who'd downed anchor with no wind in his favour. He then settled for a dream – knowing it was only a dream – that

144

he would at some point live facing the sea, in a house of wood and tile always exposed to the smell of the brine. In that propitious house he'd write a book – a simple, moving story about love and friendship – and devote his afternoons, after his siesta in the long porch open to breezes and dust clouds, to casting lines into the water and reflecting, as now, as the waves splashed his ankles, on the mysteries of the sea.

The cold water and persistent wind, less hot on the coast, the tireless waves and sun already descending on a corner of the horizon, had perhaps kept the faithful away, and the Count didn't find the colony of drop-outs he'd expected on that inhospitable rocky beach, as peripheral and forlorn as its usual clientele. Two couples went on making love in the sea at the wrong temperature and rhythm, and a group of youths skinny as stray dogs chatted next to some shrubs.

"They must be drop-outs, right, Conde?" Manolo asked when the lieutenant came out of the sea and returned to the rock.

"I expect so. It's not a good day for a swim. Better if you come to philosophize."

"Drop-outs are no philosophers, Conde, don't try that one."

"In their own way, they are, Manolo. They don't want to change the world, but try to change life, and they start with themselves. They couldn't care less about anything,

145

or almost anything, and that's the philosophy they try to transfer into praxis. I swear by my mother it sounds like a philosophical system."

"Tell that to the drop-outs. Hey, aren't drop-outs just hippies?"

"Yes, but a postmodern variety."

Manolo gave the chief his shoes back and sat down next to him, looking out to the sea.

"What did you expect to find here, Conde?"

"I've really no idea, Manolo. Perhaps a reason to smoke pot or snort a line of coke and feel that life is on a headier level. When I sit down like this and look at the sea, I sometimes think I'm living the wrong life, that it's one big nightmare, and I'm about to wake up but can't open my eyes. A load of shit, right? I'd really like to talk to these drop-outs, though I know they won't tell me anything new."

"Shall we give it a go?"

The Count looked at the youths on the coast and the couples still clasped together in the water. He tried to dry his feet on his hands and moved his fingers as if he were blowing a trumpet or a saxophone. He decided to stuff his socks in a pocket and put on his shoes.

"Off we go then."

They got up and took the best route through the rocks to get to the group talking and smoking under the high shrubs. There were four men and two women, all very young, scruffy-haired and half-starved, with a touch of grace in their eyes. Like all members of a sect they felt sectarian, because they knew they were the chosen few, or at least thought they did. Chosen by whom and why? Another philosophical issue, thought the Count, who came to a halt less than a metre away from the group.

"Can you give me a light?"

The youths, who tried to ignore the presence of the two intruders, looked at them and the one with the longest hair held out a box of matches. The Count made two abortive attempts, finally lit up and returned the matches to their owner.

"Would you like a cigarette?" he followed up, and the long-haired guy smiled.

"Told you so, didn't I?" And he looked at his companions. "The police always try the same trick."

The Count looked at his cigarette as if he'd found it particularly satisfying, and took another puff.

"So you don't want one? Thanks for the matches. How did you tell we are police?"

One of the girls, her chest as flat as the pampas and with desperately long legs, looked up at Conde and put a finger to her nose.

"It's a smell we're familiar with. We've trained our sense of smell . . ." And she smiled, convinced of her wit.

"What do you want?" enquired Long Hair, in his putative role as tribal chieftain.

147

The Count smiled and felt strangely at ease.

"To talk to you," he replied and sat down very close to the paladin. "You're drop-outs, aren't you?"

Long Hair smiled. It was clear that he knew all the likely questions forthcoming from the policemen that pestered them now and then.

"I'll make a suggestion, Mr Policeman. As you've no reason to put us inside and as we don't like talking to police as a rule, we'll answer any three questions you care to ask, and then you can clear off. Agreed?"

The Count's group spirit stirred inside him: he could also be sectarian and as a policeman he wasn't used to accepting conditions when it came to putting questions he would blast out if necessary to extract all the answers he required. It wasn't for nothing he was a policeman and that his tribe was the one with the force and even legal sanction to repress. But he held back.

"Agreed," the Count concurred.

"Yes, we are drop-outs," stated Long Hair. "Second question."

"Why are you drop-outs?"

"Because it's what we like. Everyone's free to be whatever he wants, baseball player, cosmonaut, drop-out or police. We like being drop-outs and living as we think fit. It's no crime till the contrary is proved, true or not? We don't bother anyone, don't take anything from anyone, and don't like anyone forcing us to do anything. That's democratic, don't you reckon? You've got one left."

The Count looked longingly at the bottle of rum shoehorned into a hollow in the rock. This oracle of passive democracy was going to beat him cleanly at his own game, and he saw why Long Hair was the natural leader of that crew.

"I'd like an answer from her," and he pointed at the titless streak who smiled, flattered by this police interest that gave her a protagonist's role. "Is that agreed?"

"It's agreed," agreed Long Hair, practising his self-proclaimed democratic policies.

"What do you expect from life?" he asked, throwing his fag end seawards.

Swept up by the wind, his cigarette performed a high parabola and boomeranged back to the rocks, as if to show escape was impossible. The Count scrutinized the woman he'd questioned as she thought up a reply: if she's intelligent, the Count told himself, she will attempt to philosophize. Perhaps she'll say life is something you find though you never lost it, at a time and place that are arbitrary, with parents, relatives and even neighbours that are forced upon you. Life's one big mistake, and the saddest thing she could say, thought the Count, is that nobody can change it. At most, separate it out from everything, disconnect it from family, society and time as far as you can, and that's why they were drop-outs, you know?

149

"Should one expect anything from life?" the skinny bint said finally looking at her leader. "We expect nothing from life." And her reply struck her as so intelligent that she showed her friends the palm of her hand, like a victorious athlete, ready to receive the salutations the others granted with a smile. "Just live it and end of story," she added taking another look at the inquisitive intruder.

The Count glanced at Manolo who was standing very close to him and held out a hand so that his colleague could help him up. Back on his feet he looked down on the group. It's too hot in this country for philosophy to take seed, he told himself, as he shook his hands sticky with sand and salt water.

"That's a lie as well," said the lieutenant before looking out to the sea. "You can't even do that, although it's good to try. But you suffer when it doesn't work. Thanks for the light." He waved a hand towards the group and patted Manolo on the back. As they walked away from the coast, the Count thought for a second that he felt cold. Mysteries of the sea and life always left him cold.

He too lived in an old rambling house in La Víbora, with a high roof and large windows behind grilles that started at ground level and disappeared into the higher regions. Through the open door you could see a long, dark, cool passageway, ideal for the middle of the day, that led to a tree-filled yard. The Count had to step inside to reach the door knocker which he rapped a couple of times. He went back to the porch and waited. A girl around ten years old, tense like a ballerina interrupted mid-dance, emerged from the first room to inspect the visitor.

"Is José Luis in?" asked the lieutenant and the girl, without saying a word, turned round and pirouetted back inside. Three minutes passed, and the Count was about to give the knocker another rap, when he saw the fragile figure of José Luis approaching down the corridor. The Count primed a welcoming smile.

"How are you, José Luis? Do you remember me, from the lavatory at Pre-Uni?"

The youth wiped his hand across his naked chest where too many ribs stood out. Perhaps he was hesitating before deciding to admit he remembered.

"Yes, of course. How can I help?"

The Count took out a packet of cigarettes and offered the youth one.

"I need to talk to you. It's a long time since I had any friends in that place and I think you could probably help me."

"Help in what way?"

He's as suspicious as a cat. He's the kind who knows what he wants or at least what he doesn't want, thought Conde.

151

"You're a lot like my best friend at Pre-Uni. We called him Skinny Carlos, I think he was even skinnier than you are. But he's not skinny anymore."

José Luis stepped out and into the porch.

"What is it you want to know?"

"Can we talk here?" asked the Count, pointing to the low wall separating the porch from the garden.

José nodded and the policeman was the first to sit down.

"I'll be frank and I want you be frank with me as well," the Count suggested, deliberately not looking at him to avoid any response at this stage. "I've spoken to several people about Lissette, your teacher. You and some people spoke very well of her; others said she was on the wild side. I don't know if you know how she was killed: they strangled her when she was drunk after beating her and having sex with her. Someone also smoked marijuana that night at her place."

Only then did he look the youth in the eye. The Count felt he'd made an impact.

"What do you want me to tell you?"

"What you and your friends thought about Lissette."

The youth smiled. He threw his half-smoked cigarette in the direction of the garden and returned to his rib count.

"What we thought? Is that what you're after? Look, pal, I'm seventeen, but I wasn't born yesterday. You want me to tell you what I think and put myself in the shit? That's a fool's game, if you'll forgive the expression. I've got a year and a bit left at Pre-Uni and I want to end on a high, you know? That's why I repeat that she was a good teacher and that she helped us a lot."

"You're pushing your luck, José Luis. Just remember one thing: I'm a policeman and I don't like people spending all day prevaricating with me. I think I like you, but don't get the wrong side of me because I can be real hard. Why did you answer me that day in the lavatories?"

The boy swung a leg nervously. Like the Skinny of old.

"Because you asked. And I told you what anyone could have said."

"Are you afraid?" asked the Count looking him in the eye.

"Common sense. I told you I wasn't born yesterday. Don't complicate life for me."

"All of a sudden nobody wants complications. Why don't you dare?"

"What's in it for me if I dare?"

The Count shook his head. If he was a cynic, as Candito had said, then what was this kid?

"I really had high hopes you'd help me. Perhaps because you're like my friend Skinny from when I was at Pre-Uni. Why are you acting like this?"

153

The youth looked serious and now shook his leg more quickly, stroking himself again around his sternum that divided his chest like a keel.

"Because it's the only way to act. I'll tell you something: When I was in sixth grade my school was inspected. A dad had said that our teacher hit us and they were investigating to see if it was true. They wanted someone apart from that dad and his boy to say it was true. Because it was true: that teacher was the worst bastard you can imagine. He belted us for pleasure. He used to walk in between the rows of desks and if he saw you with one foot on the desk in front, for example, he'd kick you in the leg with those boots of his . . . And, of course, nobody said anything. Everybody was scared. But I did: I said he abused us and kicked us, slapped us round the head, pulled our ears when we didn't know something and thwacked more than one face with his register. He did it to me. Naturally, the teacher got the boot, justice was done, and another new teacher came. A really nice guy. He didn't hit or hurt us . . . At the end of the year two people in the class didn't pass: the boy who first kicked up a fuss and myself. What do you reckon?"

The Count remembered himself in Pre-Uni: so what would he have done? Would he speak to that unknown policeman he had no reason to trust, beyond the simple notion that he wanted justice to be done? And what if that was how justice was done? He took out his packet of cigarettes again and gave one to skinny José Luis.

154

"Don't worry, son. Look, here's my number, at home, and if anything comes to mind, give me a ring. This is more serious than a slap round the head or an ear-pull. Remember that . . . Otherwise, I think you're right to be scared. But the fear's of your making. I hope you pass without any problems," he said and held the lit match out to José Luis's cigarette, but didn't light his: his mouth tasted unmistakeably of shit.

"Hey, Jose, I need your help."

As usual, the front door was open to the wind, the light and visitors, and Josefina was spending Saturday afternoon in front of the television screen. Her taste in television – like her son's in music – covered a range that included every possibility: whatever films they showed, even Soviet war films and martial arts films from Hong Kong; then soaps, soaps galore, whether Brazilian, Mexican, or Cuban, and whatever the theme, romance, slavery, working-class struggle or high society drama. Then, music, the news, adventures and puppets. To clock up more television she even swallowed Nitza Villapol's cookery programmes, for the pleasure of finding fault when she spotted missing ingredients or pointless extras in some of the expert's recipes. She was now watching the week's repeats of Brazilian soap and that's why the Count dared interrupt her. The woman listened to the cry for help from the

155

Count who'd sat next to her, and concluded: "Just what my father used to say: when a white man looks for a black you bet it's to fuck him up. So what's wrong, my love?"

The Count smiled and wondered whether he'd made the right decision.

"I've a real problem, Jose . . ."

"The new girlfriend?"

"Hey, dear, you hit bulls-eye."

"But you lot shout it to the heavens . . ."

"Well, she's says she's always lived round the corner, at number 75. But I've never seen her and Skinny's never heard of her. Give me a hand. Find out who she is, where she's from, anything you can."

The woman started swaying on her chair again and looked at the screen. The heroine in the soap was having a lousy time. Fine, thought Conde, that's the price you pay for being a heroine in a soap.

"Did you get that, Jose?" the Count then insisted, craving the attention he thought he'd lost.

"Yes, I got you . . . And what if you don't like what I find out? Hey, Condesito, let me tell you something. You know you're my son too and that I'll find out what you want to know. I'll act like a policeman. But you're making a mistake. I'll tell you that for nothing."

"Don't worry. You help me. I need some badly . . . And is the little fellow awake yet?"

156

"I think he's listening to music on his headset. He just asked me if you'd rung . . . There's some fried rice for you in the pot on the stove."

"Hell, you really are my mother," said the Count and, after kissing her on the forehead, he started to ruffle her hair. "But remember I want that info."

The Count entered his friend's room, a plate in one hand and a chunk of bread in the other. His back to the door, his gaze lost in the foliage of the banana trees, Skinny was singing very quietly the songs he was listening to on his headset. The Count made an effort but couldn't identify the tune.

He sat on the bed behind the wheelchair and, after lifting the first spoonful to his lips, kicked the wheel nearest to him.

"Say something, savage."

"You've put me on the scrap heap," Skinny protested, as he took off his headset and slowly swung round the chair he was sentenced to.

"Don't gripe, Skinny, it was one day I didn't call on you. Yesterday life got very hectic."

"You could have rung. Things must be going well: look at the bags under your eyes. So? Did you dance her?"

"We danced, but I didn't get to dance her. But look," he said, pointing to his shirt pocket, "I've got her here."

"I'm happy for your sake," said Carlos, and the Count noted a lack of enthusiasm in that declaration of happiness. He knew Skinny was thinking how a relationship like that would deprive him of nights and Sundays in the Count's company, and the Count also knew his friend was right, because at root nothing had changed between them: they continued to be possessive, like insecure adolescents.

"Don't have a go, Skinny, it's not the end of the world."

"I really am happy for you, you beast. You need a woman and I hope you've just found one."

The Count put down his plate that looked as if it had been washed clean and flopped onto Skinny's bed, glancing at the old posters on the wall.

"I think this is it. I'm in love like a dog, like a mongrel. My defences are all down: I don't know how I can fall in love like this. But she's beautiful, savage, and intelligent."

"You're exaggerating. Beautiful *and* intelligent? Hey, you're talking a load of shit."

"I swear by your mother she is. If it's a lie, she needn't save any more fried rice for me."

"So, how come you didn't lay her?"

"She told me to wait, that it was too soon."

"You see, she can't be that intelligent. How can she resist the ardour of a brilliant, handsome good dancer like you? I mean . . ."

"Just go to hell, will you? You know, Skinny, I'm fucking worried. That night, after listening to Andrés, I couldn't stop thinking about what he said. I know he was half drunk, but he spoke with feeling. And now something really upsetting has just happened to me."

"What's that, brother?" he asked, knitting his brows. In the old days he'd have swung his leg when asking a question like that, the Count told himself, as he recalled his conversation with José Luis.

"Can I tell you something, savage?" asked Carlos, as he interrupted the movement he was about to make in his chair. "If you put yourself in the skinny kid's place you'll realize that basically he's right. Remember one thing: a school is often like a prison, and he who talks, loses out. The pay-off for the piper. He'll have a reputation for being a snitch the rest of his life. Would you have talked? I don't really think so. But though he didn't talk, he gave you a crumb: something or everything's up. The marijuana scene, the teacher's affair with the head and God knows what else. That's why he didn't talk, because he knows something, or at least imagines he does. He's no cynic, Conde, it's the law of the jungle. What's terrible is that there's a jungle and it's got a law . . . Look at yourself: you spend your life remembering. Don't you recall how you knew about that fraud when the Water-Pre scandal broke and you shut up like the rest and you even went into the exams knowing all the answers in advance? Didn't you know that when they came to paint Pre-Uni they stole half the paint and so couldn't paint

159

inside the classrooms? And don't you remember how we won all the banners and all the competitions in the sugar cane because there was an insider in the warehouse who gave us sacks that weren't ours? Have you forgotten all that? Hell, what a policeman. My friend, you can't live on nostalgia. Nostalgia deceives: it only reminds you of what you want to remember and that can be very healthy at times, but it's almost always counterfeit currency. But, you know, I don't reckon you've ever been fit for life. You're beyond the pale. You fucking live in the past. Live your life now, guy. It's not such a sin. No kidding . . . You know, I don't often talk about it, but I sometimes start thinking about what happened to me in Angola, and I see myself back in that hole under the ground, three or four days without a wash and eating a mouthful of sardine and rice, sleeping with my face stuck in that dust smelling of dried fish that's all over Angola, and I think it's incredible anyone can live like that: because what's curious, is that it didn't kill us off. Nobody died from that and you learned something existed like another life, another history, that had nothing to do with all we were going through. That's why it was easier to go mad than die, stuck in those holes, without the slightest fucking idea how long it would be for and not once seeing the face of your enemy, who might be any of the people we met in the villages we passed through. It was horrific, brother, and what's more we knew we were there to die, because it was war, and it was a lottery and you might strike lucky and get the number to get out alive: it was that simple, and totally out of your hands. So it was better not to remember. And those who forgot everything resisted best: if there was no water they couldn't wash, spent three or four days without washing their face or teeth and even ate stones if they could soften them up and never said they were expecting letters or talked about how they were going to die or were going to be saved, they knew there were going to be saved. Not me, I acted like you, shit full of nostalgia, and I'd start reckoning up how I'd got there, why the hell I was in that hole, until I got shot up and then they did take me out. I got my bloody number in the lottery all right, didn't I? I don't know why you force me to remember all that. I don't like remembering because I was a loser, but when I do think about it, like now, I draw two very clear conclusions: Rabbit is a bastard if he thinks that history can be re-written, and I'm fucked, as Andrés says, but all the same I want to keep living and you know it. And you know you're my friend and that I need you, but I'm not so selfish to want you to be fucked here next to me. And you also know that it doesn't make sense for you to spend your life blaming everyone else and blaming yourself . . . The skinny lad is probably a cynic, as you say, but try to understand him, pal. Come on, solve this case, find out what happened at Pre-Uni and do what

161

you have to do although it pains your soul. Then shag Karina and fall in love if you have to and enjoy it, laugh and screw, and if it all goes pear-shaped, take the pain, but keep living, because we have to, right?"

"I think so."

"Huh, I'll be waiting on the steps at Pre-Uni, at seven? At seven then, and don't bring the car," he'd said, with the morbid, premeditated idea of a possible journey into the world of melancholy. Skinny can go to hell, he told himself, he'd agreed his last love date seventeen years ago in that place that constantly hit at him from past and present, like a magnetic pole of memory and reality he couldn't and didn't want to escape. He was all set to dive into a swimming pool overflowing with nostalgia.

He got there at a quarter to seven and, between the reddish light of dusk and the lamps on the high plinth of the columns, he tried to read the day's paper while waiting. Sometimes weeks went by without him stopping to read the paper, he checked out the headlines and ditched it without remorse or hesitation: he wasn't at all gone on the idea of wasting precious minutes devouring news and comment that was self-evident. What might Caridad Delgado be writing about three days after her daughter's death? He should look out for that newspaper. The wind had died down; he could open the pages of the daily as he had nothing better on offer. The front page informed him that the sugar campaign was progressing slowly but surely to another record of success and high figures; Soviet cosmonauts were still in space, breaking new records for staying up, indifferent to the disturbing pages of international news that spoke of the degeneration of their – previously so perfect – country, and oblivious to the war to the death unleashed between Armenians and Azeris; tourism in Cuba was marching – and this was a perfectly chosen verb – in giant strides, and had already tripled hotel capacity; for their part, workers in the culinary arts and services in the capital had already begun their arduous inter-municipal struggle to win the right to be provincial host for the 4 February celebrations, the Day for Workers in their trade: to that end they'd implemented initiatives and improved the quality of their services and striven to eradicate lacunae, that kind of ontological fatality the Count thought was a beautifully poetic way to describe the most basic of thefts. Then, no change in the Middle East: it got worse and worse, everything was getting shittier and on course for outright war; violence was on the increase in the United States; there were more disappearances in Guatemala, more murders in El Salvador, more unemployed in Argentina and more destitute in Brazil. Didn't I just land on a wonderful planet? What was a teacher's death among so many deaths? Could Long Hair and his tribe be right? And then, the baseball league was advancing

163

– a less sporting synonym for marching – towards the final strait with Havana in the lead; Pipín was about to beat his own record for apnoea immersion (and he recalled he was always promising to look that word up in the dictionary, perhaps there existed a less horrible synonym?). He closed the newspaper convinced that everything was marching, advancing or continuing on schedule and turned his mind to contemplating the sunset, also on schedule for that exact moment, 18.52, normal time. As he observed the sun's rapid descent he thought he would like to write something about the emptiness of existence: not about death or failure or disillusion, only emptiness. A man facing the void. It would be worthwhile if he could find a good character. Could he himself be that character? Sure he could, recently he'd been feeling too much self-pity and the result might be more than perfect: the entire darkness revealed, the entire void in a single individual . . . But that can't be, he told himself, I'm waiting for a woman and I feel fine, I'm going to shaft her and we'll get drunk.

Only he was a policeman and, although he sometimes thought he wasn't, he always thought like a policeman. He was in the territory of his own melancholy, but also in the domains of Lissette Núñez Delgado, and he thought that the void and death seemed too alike and that death in the singular, even on a planet strewn with corpses that had been more or less foreseen, still weighed as a risk on

164

the scales of that most necessary equilibrium: life. Only six days before, perhaps sitting on that same step on those stairs, a twenty-four year-old girl, full of the desire to live, might have enjoyed the beauty of that splendid sunset, oblivious to the world's wars and the anguish of a record apnoea, looking forward to the new pair of trainers she would soon own. Now nothing remained of the hopes and upsets of that woman: perhaps the memory with which she marked that building inhabited by millions of other memories, like his own; perhaps the amorous frustrations and even possible guilt of a head teacher who felt rejuvenated, perhaps the uncertainty of pupils who thought they'd pass in chemistry with ease thanks to that unusual teacher. By 18.53 the sun had sunk into the world's end – like memory – leaving in its wake the light from its last rays.

Then he saw her advancing under the blossoming *majaguas* and felt his life filling up, like his lungs, replete with the air and scents of spring, and he forgot about the void and death, the sun and nothingness: she could be everything, he thought, as he walked down the steps of Pre-Uni at the double and met a kiss and body that clung to his like a promise of the most desired, close encounter of the first kind.

"What's your opinion of nostalgia?"

"That it was invented by writers of boleros."

"And apnoea immersion?"

165

"That it is unnatural."

"And haven't you ever been told you're the most beautiful woman in La Víbora?"

"I've heard the odd comment."

"And that a good policeman's after you?"

"I realized that, from the interrogations," she said and they kissed again, in the middle of the street, as shameless as adolescents in full flood.

"Do you like being wooed in parks?"

"It's a long time since I've been wooed in a park. Or anywhere."

"Which park do you prefer in La Víbora? Take your pick: Córdoba, Los Chivos, either of those on San Mariano, the Parque del Pescao, the one in Santos Suárez, on Mónaco, the one with the lion cubs in Casino and the one on Acosta . . . The best thing about this barrio are its parks, the most beautiful in Havana."

"Are you sure?"

"More than sure. Which do you fancy?"

She looked him in the eye and ruminated. The Count lost himself in the depths of her eyes like an infatuated policeman.

"If you're only going to woo me, I'd prefer the one on Mónaco. If you've got itchy fingers, then the Parque del Pescao."

"Let it be the Parque del Pescao then. I'll not be held responsible for myself."

166

"And why don't you invite me to your place?"

She surprised him, anticipated an invitation he'd not dared to issue when they spoke on the phone and confirmed his suspicion that this woman was a woman and a half and there was no point in beating about the bush. Like Tarzan lusting after Jane.

"I ignored what you said," she said with a smile. "I parked the car on the corner. Will you or won't you invite me? I like the coffee you brew."

His hands shook as he united the two halves of the coffee pot. He was disturbed by the intimacy of love as intensely as in the old days of amorous initiation and he improvised on themes that flowed easily: the secrets about coffee he had learned from Josefina; "we must go and see my best friend Skinny and her, I can't understand how you've never met," and he peered at his coffee pot to see whether percolation had begun, "they live round the corner from your house"; his preference for Chinese cuisine, Sebastian Wong, "the father of Patricia, a colleague at headquarters, prepares some amazing soups"; the idea for a story he wanted to write, on solitude and emptiness . . . He poured the first drops of coffee in the jug where he'd put two small spoonfuls of sugar which he beat into an ochre, caramelized paste; "while I was waiting for you I thought about writing something along those lines, I've been wanting to write for several days," and he poured the remaining coffee into the jug and yellow, probably bitter foam formed on the top, and he poured it into two big cups and announced, "Espresso coffee," as he sat down opposite her. "Whenever I fall in love I think I can write again."

"Do you fall in love so quickly?"

"I don't always linger so."

"Love of literature or of women?"

"A fear of loneliness. A panic attack. Is the coffee to your liking?"

She nodded and looked at the window and the night.

"What have you found out about the dead girl?"

"Not much: she expected too much from life, was able and ambitious and changed boyfriends as often as her bras."

"And what does that mean?"

"She was what the ancients and some moderns would call a little whore."

"Why did she change boyfriends? Is that what you think about women? Are you the kind that would like to marry a virgin?"

"That's what every Cuban man aspires to, I suppose? I don't aim so high now: I'll settle for a redhead."

She gave no sign she accepted his compliment and finished her coffee.

"And if the redhead was a little whore?"

He smiled and shook his head, indicating she'd misunderstood.

"I said little whore because that's what she was: she could go to bed with a man for a pair of shoes," he explained and regretted telling her the truth: he wanted to bed her and intended to give her a pair of shoes, in fact. "I'm only interested in her changes of boyfriend as a policeman: that may be why she was killed. The dead have no privacy."

"It's incredible, isn't it? That they can kill someone, like that, on any pretext?"

The Count smiled and finished his coffee. He lit the cigarette, his mouth urgently craving that complement to the enduring taste of the infusion.

"It's what usually happens. Someone is killed for no real reason, probably on the spur of the moment. It's often a mistake: criminals prefer not to murder but sometimes cross that line because they can't avoid it. It's a chemical chain reaction . . . I feed on such incontinence. It's sad, isn't it?"

She nodded and then took the offensive: she stretched her hand across the dark formica table top and took the forearm of the man who seemed to relish sadness, and started caressing it. A woman who knows how to caress, he thought, not a phantom passing . . .

"Oh, how beautiful you are, my love, how beautiful you are! Your eyes are like doves!"

He declaims biblically like Solomon, when, feeling as beautiful as Jerusalem, she abandons her coffee and chair and advances on him, never letting go of his arm, and pulls his mouth down to her breasts – like twin gazelles "that graze among the lilies" – so with his free hand he can fumble to undo her blouse and find himself not before two gazelles, but warm, wild tits, with ripe plum nipples that stir anxiously at the first flickering touch of his reptilian tongue, and, a baby again, he sucks, starting a journey to the origins of life and the world.

He penetrates her slowly, as if afraid to shed a petal, sitting on his chair, picking her up by the waist, light and amenable, lowering her on to his pole, like a sacred banner in need of protection against the rain and dusk. Her first cry takes him by surprise, she arches between his hands as if wounded by a silver bullet shattering her heart, then he hugs her tighter to feel the black forest of her magic triangle on his pubes, and lowers his hands to her buttocks to run over the perfect furrow dividing them ands lets his eager finger run unhurriedly, never pausing, from anus to vulva, from vulva to anus, carrying wet heat, feeling the urgent thickness at the root of his penis, rigid and prickly as it drilled, and the padded softness of her opulent, knowing lips that suck him like eager quicksand, and then he lets his finger wander between the folds of her anus and feels the louder cry provoked by the double penetration now becoming triple

170

with the savage tongue that tries to silence her, when all silence is impossible, because the deep sluices are open and the deepest rivers of their desires flow to a glory on an earth that has been recovered. The renascent gusts of the Lenten wind wrap them in tight embrace.

"You'll be the death of me," are the words of love he articulates.

"I'll be the death of myself," she laments, as she shivers all vulnerable, perhaps because of the wind, perhaps because of the moral and physical certainty of consummation.

Several days later, while ruminating on the tangible opportunities that come policemen's way – to find happiness and change their lives – Detective Lieutenant Mario Conde began to grasp the real extent of that suicide on a well-ridden saddle . . . But he can't think now, because Karina dismounts as if levitating and, rescuing the pants still hanging from one of the Count's thighs, she cleans the spume from his penis and, kneeling like a penitent, swallows it as if she'd been starving for days and now it's the Count who cries out, "Fuck, cunt," the words he utters, astounded by the beauty of the prostrated woman whose head he can barely see, that says yes and yes again, with total conviction, and a reddish hair that opens up in the centre of the head in an unexpected cleft. While his penis begins to grow beyond what is possible, unimaginable, even permissible, the Count feels himself

171

powerful, animal, in full possession of his senses, until dictator-like he exercises the power he has been given, takes the woman's head in his hands and forces her to hit bottom and beyond, until he pours into her throat, that prisoner under sentence, an ejaculation he feels descend from the innermost reaches of his brain. You'll be the death of me. I'll be the death of myself . . . They kiss, on the brink.

I came across a quite unexpected façade yesterday. I must have passed that hitherto anodyne, filthy spot on the 10th October Avenue a thousand times, by the street corner which harboured the cockpit where Grandfather Rufino had, eight times, put his fortune on spurs that enriched and impoverished him in equal measure. But yesterday for the first time an alarm bell, specially aimed at my brain, forced me to look up and there it was, waiting for me from time immemorial: in the middle of a roughly classical triangle, the coat-of-arms of a well-to-do Creole, atop a building that wasn't at all well-to-do, worn by time and rain. Only the date remained mysteriously intact: 1919, on the chipped eave, under the battered shield. At the vortex of two cornucopias hurling tropical fruit into the air, the inevitable pineapples, soursops and anones, mangos and furtive avocados, no soft fruit, meat or greens, and where others would have placed castles or fields of azure, a prodigious

172

canebrake to which the date, architectural wealth and fruit-filled shield necessarily paid tribute, to its source . . . I love discovering these unpredictable heights of Havana – second and third floors, out-of-date baroque, bereft of spiritual contortions, names of owners long forgotten, cemented dates and glass skylights broken by stones, balls and the passage of time – where I always thought there was an air path to the sky. At that height, beyond human reach, exists the purest soul of the city that further down is tarnished by sordid, heartbreaking stories. Havana has been a city in its own right for two centuries and imposes its own laws and selects its own adornments to mark its unique resilience. Why was this city, this proud, exuberant city fated to be mine? I try to understand this fate I can't throw off, that I didn't choose, as I try to understand the city, but Havana eludes me, always takes me by surprise with its forlorn black-and-white photo shots and my perception is as worn and cracked as the old coat-of-arms of those who luxuriated on wealth from mangos, pineapples and sugar. After so much rapture and rejection, my relationship with the city has been marked by a chiaroscuro painted by my eyes: the pretty young girl turned sad hooker, an angry man a potential murderer, the petulant youth an incurable drug addict, the old man on the corner a thief wanting peace. Everything blackens over time, like the city where I pace, between crumbling arches, petrified

173

rubbish tips, walls peeled to the bone, drains overflowing like rivers born in the heart of hell and rocky balconies living on props. In the end the city that chose me, and I, the chosen one, resemble each other: we die a little each day, a long, premature death made from pinpricks, pain that is progressive, tumours that advance . . . And although I want to rebel, this city grips me by the neck and overwhelms me with its arcane mysteries. That's why I realize the decrepit beauty of a well-to-do coat-of-arms and a city's apparent peace are transient and mortal – a city I know I see through the eyes of love, that dares show me those unexpected delights from its sumptuous past. I'd like to be able to see the city through your eyes, she told me when I described my recent find, and I think it would be melancholically beautiful – perhaps, squalid and moving – to show her my city, but I know it's impossible, for she could never wear my spectacles, as she's beside herself with happiness, and the city will never reveal itself to her. Miller said Paris is like a whore, but Havana is more whorish: she only offers herself up to those who repay her in pain and anguish, and even then she doesn't yield up her whole self, doesn't surrender the innermost secrets from her entrails.

"The most solid proof of Jesus's authority is that he didn't need distance to wield it but exercised it from the closest proximity to his neighbour. Power dresses

174

itself in attributes (wealth, might, banking knowledge) that constitute its glory as it simultaneously creates remoteness. The powerful, when naked, feel impotent, but Jesus, the son of man, naked and barefoot, lived among men, remained among them and exercised over them the infinite sweetness of his infinite power . . ."

Always the infinite, the infinitely invariable, and the dilemma of power, thought the Count, who had last seen the inside of a church on the memorable day of his first communion. He'd prepared at Sunday catechism over many a month for that act of religious re-affirmation that he had to go through, knowing full well why: he would receive, from the priest's hands, a small piece of flour that contained the whole essence of the great (infinite) mystery; the immortal soul and suffering body of Our Lord Jesus Christ (with all his power) would pass from his mouth to his (equally) immortal soul. This would be a necessary digestive step to possible salvation or the most terrible damnation, he now knew, and the knowledge transformed him into an (infinitely) responsible being. Nevertheless, at the age of seven the Count thought he knew a lot of other things much better: that Sunday was the best day for playing the best games of baseball outside his house, for going off to steal mangos from Genaro's farm, for taking a bike ride – two or even three on each bike – to fish *biajacas* and swim in the Chorrerra river. Consequently, though delighted to dress him smartly in white so he could take his communion, the Count's mother then seethed with an anger prohibited by the communion itself, as she heard the boy's final word: he wanted to idle around on Sunday mornings and would not be going back to church.

The Count couldn't imagine his return to a parish church, almost thirty years after defecting, would spark off the feeling he'd suddenly recovered a quiescent, not simply lost memory: the cavernous smell of the chapel, the tall shadows from the domes, the reflections of a sun dimmed by stained glass, the blurry glints from the main altar were all present in his memory of that poor, small-scale church in his barrio. Such memories were tangible in the inevitably luxurious church of the Passionists, with its Creole neo-Gothic finery, the highest domes decorated with filigree, celestial gold, the sensation of the smallness of humans provoked by a structure reaching for heaven and a profusion of hyper-realistic, human-sized images and gestures of resignation that seemed about to speak; became tangible in the church he'd now entered, in the middle of the mass, searching for the saviour he needed right now, namely Red Candito.

When Cuqui told him that Candito was in church the Count's first reaction was one of surprise. It was the first he'd heard about Red's profession of faith, but he was pleased, for he could talk to him on neutral territory. In front of that façade with towers like exotic European pines, the policeman had hesitated for a second about what he should do: but then decided to wait for Candito by participating in the mass himself. Conde breathed in the pliant smell of cheap incense; he sat on the back pew and listened to the Sunday sermon of that priest who was young and vigorous in his gestures and words, and spoke to his flock of the most arcane mysteries, of power and the infinite, in the tones of a good conversationalist:

"The paternity of Jesus, who revealed the paternity of God through fraternal solidarity. By relating to people from below, at their level, he not only saved the one who received the gospel, and Jesus was fulfilled as brother to men and as son of God. Hence the vulnerability of Jesus: his joy when simple people welcomed the revelation of God and his sorrow for Jerusalem, because of the authorities that wouldn't receive him . . ."

Then the priest raised his arms and the parishioners who packed his church stood up. Feeling he was profaning an arcane mystery he himself had renounced, the Count took advantage of that movement to escape like a man persecuted into the light of the square, a cigarette between his lips and an amen in his ears chorused by people who were happy once again to have known the sacrifices made by their Lord.

Fifteen minutes later the believers began to process, their faces lit by an inner light rivalling the splendour

177

of the Sunday sun. Red Candito, on the last step of the stairs, stopped to light a cigarette and greeted an old black guy who was walking by, dressed in a linen guayabera and straw hat, perhaps in flight from a 1920s photo. The Count waited in the middle of the square, and saw how his friend raised his eyebrows when he spotted him.

"I didn't know you were a churchgoer," the Count said, shaking his hand.

"Some Sundays," admitted Candito who suggested they should cross the road. "It makes me feel good."

"Church depresses me. What do you hope to find there, Candito?"

The mulatto smiled, as if the Count had said something stupid.

"What I can't find elsewhere . . ."

"Of course, the infinite. You know, I now find myself surrounded by mystics."

Candito smiled again.

"And what's up now, Conde?"

They walked up Vista Alegre and the Count waited for his breathing to settle after their climb as the ochre structure of the school where Lissette Núñez had taught and where they had met came into sight.

"Yesterday I was thinking this bastard Pre-Uni seems to wield power over my destiny. I can't throw it off."

"They were good years."

178

"I think they were the best, Red, but it's not as simple as that. This is where we grew up, right? It was here I met most of the people who are my friends. You, for example."

"I'm sorry about Friday, Conde, but you've got to understand me . . ."

"I do, I do, Candito. There are things you can't ask of people. But a twenty-four year-old woman was teaching in one of the classrooms over there until she turned up the other day dead, murdered, and I've got to find out who did it. It is that simple. And I've got to find out for several reasons: because I'm a policeman, because the person who did it must be called to account, because she was a Pre-Uni teacher . . . It's a fucking obsession."

"What about Pupy?"

"It looks as if it wasn't him, although we're putting the screws on him. He told us something important: the head of Pre-Uni was having an affair with her."

"Didn't he do it then?"

"I'm off to see him now, but he's got a good alibi."

"So what do you reckon?"

"That if the head isn't the solution then marijuana can probably give me a lead."

Candito lit another cigarette. They were level with the PE yard and from the street they could see the basketball court, its bare hoops and boards worn out by all those hard throws. The playground was empty, like every Sunday, a sad place without the hue-and-cry from

179

matches, the rivalries and girls reduced to hysteria by a brilliant shot.

"Do you remember who used to score the most?"

"Marcos Quijá," answered the Count.

"Piss off," protested Candito with a smile. "I taught Marcos how to dribble. You know, in one game, I scored two from the halfway line against those jerks from Vedado."

"If you say so . . ."

"Look, Conde," said Candito, stopping on the street corner, where a stinking overflow trickled from a rubbish container that was new there, "things have changed. In our day if anyone smoked marijuana it was because he was an addict, but now anyone can get dope and that's when the trouble starts because they all go crazy. The same with rum: before you did or you didn't, now any one can, and there's no such thing as a nice girl, because shagging is the order . . . But I can tell you something I heard yesterday that may help . . . and remember I'm risking my neck. I don't know if it's true or not, but I heard there's a fellow who lives in Casino Deportivo, I don't know where exactly, but you can find that out, who's been shifting red-hot dope for days. Nobody knows where it came from, but it's red-hot. He's known as Lando the Russian . . . See where that takes you. But let me be for two years, Conde, OK?"

The Count took Candito by the arm and gently forced him to walk along.

180

"And what do I do to buy some size-five sandals from you?"

"Well, you can take the sandals now, and then start counting the two years you won't see me . . ."

"And in all that time you won't invite me for a drink?"

"Piss off, Conde."

"What have you stirred up now, Conde?" asked the Boss not stirring from his seat behind his desk.

"I'll tell you in a second. Just let me say hello to our comrade," he raised his arms, as if appealing for respite from a demanding judge of good manners, and shook hands with Captain Cicerón who was sitting in one of the big armchairs. They greeted each other with the usual smiles and the Count asked: "Does it still hurt?"

"Just a little," replied the captain.

Three years ago Captain Ascensio Cicerón had been designated head of the Drugs Section at headquarters. He was a dark-skinned mulatto, with a constant smile on his lips and a widespread reputation as a good person. The Count only had to see him to remember that fateful baseball game: they had met in their university days and played together in the faculty team in 1977, and Cicerón had become famous as the result of a fly that had dropped on his head, the only day they gave him a glove and he went out to cover second base, with more enthusiasm than skill. There were never enough baseball players in their faculty of artists and thinkers, and Cicerón accepted the role assigned to him by his rank-and-file committee: he'd be a member of the team for the Caribbean Games. Luckily, when the wretched fly-ball fell on Cicerón's head they were already losing by twelve to one and their manager, resigned to the inevitable, just shouted at him from the bench: "Get up, mulatto, we're catching up". Ever since the Count had greeted him with a smile and the same question.

The lieutenant sat in the other armchair and looked at his boss: "It's looking good," he commented.

"I imagine so, because on this particular Sunday I'd not intended putting in an appearance, and Cicerón started his holidays yesterday, so make sure it is really good."

"You tell me . . . Let's go from the simple to the sophisticated, as the song goes . . . We checked out the head teacher's alibi and it's just as he said, but it could be total fabrication. According to his wife, he spent the whole night at home writing a report while she watched a film. And the report in fact exists, but he could easily have drawn it up the day before and then dated it Tuesday the eighteenth. It is true, however, that this fun will cost him his marriage. The man's fucked himself. Well, when I was talking to Pupy it slipped out that Lissette had a Mexican boyfriend a few months ago. The detail seemed significant as people reckon the marijuana isn't

Cuban. Now this afternoon one Mauricio Schwartz, the only Mexican Mauricio doing the tourist bit in Cuba these days is going back to Mexico. We've organized a photograph so Pupy can identify him. If it's the same man it wouldn't be a surprise if he'd come back to see Lissette . . . What else . . . Best of all I have a name and a lead that may be real dynamite," he said looking at Cicerón. "The report on the marijuana that appeared in Lissette Núñez's house says that it wasn't any ordinary dope, that it must be Mexican or Nicaraguan, am I right?"

"Yes, I told you that. It had been affected by water, but it's almost definite it's not local."

"And you caught two guys with joints from Central America, didn't you?"

"Yes, but I haven't been able to find out where they got it. Their so-called supplier disappeared or the guys invented a ghost."

"Well, I've got a flesh-and-blood ghost: Orlando San Juan, alias Lando the Russian. I heard a whisper he's got some really strong stuff and I bet it's the same that's round and about in town."

"And how do you know, Conde?" asked Major Rangel, who'd finally got to his feet. Like every Sunday he'd gone to headquarters not in uniform but wearing a tight-fitting pullover so he could show off his swimmer/squash player pecs intent on keeping autumn at bay.

"The word was passed on to me. A whisper doing the rounds."

"Ah, a whisper . . . And you got the file on this Russian?"

"Here it is."

"Do you want Cicerón to help you?"

"That's what friends are for, aren't they?" replied the Count looking at the captain.

"I'll help him, Major," Cicerón agreed with a smile.

"Good," said the Boss and made a gesture as if frightening hens away, "exercise keeps the cold at bay. Find that Russian and see what you can get out of him and don't stop until I tell you to. But I want to know every step you make, you listening? Because this is going all black as ants. Your antics in particular, Mario Conde."

Casino Deportivo seemed varnished by the Sunday sun. All clean, painted and gleaming in technicolour. Pity I don't like this barrio anymore, the Count told himself now in front of Lando the Russian's house. They were barely five blocks from where Caridad Delgado lived and he thought how he'd like to deduce something from that proximity. Caridad, Lissette and the Russian, all in the same bag? The lieutenant took his glasses off when Captain Cicerón came out of the house.

"Well? Turned anything up?"

"You know, Conde, Lando the Russian is no small-time dealer. A man with his record isn't going to walk the streets selling joints to dopers. And someone who deals in quantity won't keep his stock under his bed, so searching this place any more is a waste of time. I'll put out a search-and-arrest order, but if what his aunt says is true and the fellow rented a beach house, the Guanabo folk will track him down in two or three hours and don't worry because I need to get my hands on this guy more than you do. This marijuana trade is pissing me off and I need to know where it fucking came from and who brought it. I'll send Lieutenant Fabricio off right now to liaise with the Guanabo folk."

"So Fabricio is with you now, is he?" asked the Count, remembering his last encounter with the lieutenant.

"It's been a month or so. He's learning."

"Just as well . . . Hey, Cicerón, could the marijuana be from one of those lost consignments that gets thrown overboard?" asked the Count as he lit up and leaned against Captain Cicerón's official car.

"It could be, anything's possible, but what's strange is that it's fallen into the hands of people who know how to move it. And the other problem is it's not South American, which is what they sometimes try to ship past Cuba. I can't imagine how it got here, but if it was set up, they can get anything in through the same channel . . . that's why we've got to catch Lando with the goods . . ."

"Yes, we've got to, because Manolo called me on your radio to say the Mexican is a no-go. It was his first time in

Cuba and Pupy says he's not the one who went out with Lissette. So Lando is the man of the moment. And the case is over to you, right?"

Cicerón smiled. He was almost always smiling and did so now as he placed a hand on one of Conde's shoulders.

"Tell me, Mario, why did you hand me this case on a plate?"

"I told you just now, didn't I? What are friends for?"

"You know you're never going to get anywhere if you throw cases around like confetti."

"Not even if I go home and start washing all my dirty clothes?"

"You have such high aspirations."

"Well, I don't. Washing clothes is a pain in the arse. If anything crops up, you'll find me between the sink and the clothes-line," he said, shaking his friend's hand.

In the car, on his way home, the Count reflected that Casino Deportivo was a good place to live after all: from deputy ministers and journalists to marijuana dealers it had a bit of everything, like any other stretch of the Good Lord's vineyard.

The Count pegged the last pair of underpants on the clothes line and contentedly surveyed his praiseworthy labours. I must be a vanguard policeman, he told himself, watching the gusts of winds make all the clothes that

186

his hands had washed dance in the air, hands softened by water and still smelling of potash and scented conditioner: three sheets, three pillowcases and four towels, boiled and washed; two pairs of trousers, twelve shirts, six pullovers, eight pairs of socks and eleven underpants; the whole range from his wardrobe, clean and gleaming under the midday sun. It had been a must: he contemplated the fruit of his labours in ecstasy, burning to witness the miracle of the entire, aseptic drying process.

He went inside and saw it was almost 3 p.m. He heard a cry of panic rise from the darkness of his gut. It would be quite wrong to go to Josefina at that hour in the afternoon and beg for a plateful of food: he imagined her in front of her television, nodding off, yawning like a good early riser and lapping up the Sunday films, so he decided to earn himself even more merit points by preparing his own lunch. How I need you, Karina, he thought when he opened the fridge and eyed the dramatic loneliness of two possibly prehistoric eggs and a piece of bread that could easily be a survivor from the siege of Stalingrad. He dropped the two eggs in heterodox fat tasting of mutually hostile fry-ups, toasted the two slices of bread on a flame that managed to melt their heart of steel on the end of his fork. A hundred per cent socialist realism, he told himself. He downed the eggs thinking of Karina again and the date they'd agreed for tonight, but not even dreams of their meeting could temper the taste of that food. Although he sensed the daring sexual adventures of the previous day were unique and unrepeatable, full of discoveries, surprises, revelations and signs of portentous paths to explore, a second encounter, after that experience, might break all the records from his real and imaginary sexual expectations and knowledge: as he swallowed two greasy eggs with leaking yolks, the Count saw himself, on that very chair, at once the beneficiary and object of a mind-blasting fellatio that left him exhausted until, two hours later, Karina began her third victorious offensive against defences that were apparently down. And tonight she'd come, armed with her saxophone . . .

"Don't ring me, because I'll probably have to go out. I'll come at night," she'd said.

"With your saxophone?"

"Huh-huh," she said imitating the man's intonation.

The Count sang as he washed the dishes, frying pan and cups where the previous day's coffee and lusts still lingered. He'd once heard it said that only a woman who'd been well served sexually could sing as she washed up. Surreptitious machismo: simple sexual determinism, he concluded as he sang on, "Good morning, star shine, / I say hello . . ." As he dried his hands he critically surveyed the state of his flat: tiles covered in grease, dust and grime more ancient than envy didn't make his place an especially magic spot for passionate dates, saxophone included. It's the price love pays, he told himself, looking with male love at the broom and duster, preparing to present Karina a clean, well-lit haven.

It was gone four-thirty when he finished his cleaning and proudly contemplated the rebirth of that place abandoned by female hands for over two years. Even Rufino, his fighting fish, had been favoured by that overdue spring-clean and swam in clear, oxygenated waters. "You're a bastard drop-out, Rufino, you good-for-nothing . . ." The Count was so pleased with himself he even considered giving a lick of paint to walls and ceilings in the near future and putting potted plants in the right places and even getting poor Rufino a mate. I'm horribly in love, he told himself, and dialled Skinny Carlos's number.

"Listen to this, savage: I've washed my sheets, towels, shirts, pants and even two pairs of trousers and just given the house the once over."

"You're horribly in love," his friend confirmed and the Count smiled. "Have you taken your temperature? You must be in a bad way."

"And what are you up to?"

"What do you think I'm up to?"

"Watching baseball?"

"We won the first game and the second is about to start."

"Playing who?"

"The bozos from Matanzas. But the interesting games

start on Tuesday, against those fucking bastard Orientales . . . Speaking of which, Rabbit says if nothing untoward happens he'll drive us to the stadium on Tuesday. Brother, I'm dead keen to go to the stadium. Hey, are you or aren't you coming today?"

The Count glanced at his spick-and-span house and felt the hollowness left by the two fried eggs in his gut.

"I'm seeing her tonight . . . What did Jose cook for lunch?"

"You animal, you missed a treat: chicken in rice juicy enough to bring back the dead. Guess how many helpings I knocked back."

"Two?"

"Come off it, three and a half!"

"And is there any left?"

"I don't think so . . . Although I heard the old girl saying she might keep some for you . . ."

"Hey, can't you hear something?"

"What?"

"Your doorbell ringing. Tell Jose to open up, it'll be me," and he hung up.

LOVE IN THE TIMES OF CHOLERA
by Caridad Delgado

I have always defended freedom in love. The fulfilment it brings, the beauty one discovers, the anguish it can

190

usher in. But now Aids has given a bitter reminder to those of us who live in the common home that is our planet Earth, that we can remain aloof from nothing that happens anywhere: wars, nuclear tests, epidemics, let alone love. Because the world gets smaller by the day.

And although happiness is always possible in these turn-of-the-century times, a scourge is whipping love and making it a difficult, dangerous option. Aids threatens us and there is only one way to avoid it: by carefully choosing one's partner, seeking safe sex, way beyond necessary measures like the use of condoms.

My readers shouldn't think I'm trying to deliver them a moral lecture or an instant lesson in self-denial. Nor do I want to restrict the free choice of love that likes to surprise us with its mysterious, warm presence. No. And even less to use my position to interfere in matters of an entirely private nature. But the fact is that danger haunts us, whatever our sexual inclinations.

I don't aspire to reveal what has already been revealed, when I remind you that promiscuity has been the main means of transmitting the apocalyptic scourge across our planet. Consequently, I'm shocked when I talk to some people, in particular the young people my work brings me into contact with, who seem unaware of the danger implicit in certain attitudes towards life, and practise sex as if it were a simple game of cards one will

191

win or lose, for, as they sometimes say, "You've got to die from something . . ."

The Count shut his newspaper. For how long? he wondered. A promiscuous daughter had died three days ago from a motive much less novel and romantic than Aids and she was capable of writing that rubbish about *fin-de-siècle* sexual insecurities. The bitch. Right then the Count lamented his pathetic manual clumsiness. Never, not even when it was a compulsory task in class, had he managed to make a little paper aeroplane, or even a glass for drinking water or coffee, despite the efforts of the teacher he fell in love with. But he now put every effort into it, almost lovingly tore the page from the newspaper, and separated out from the article he'd just read from. He stood up, leaned slightly forward, and with the skill brought by practice wiped the striated remains of his defecation on the article with a well-honed flourish. He dropped the paper in the basket and pulled the chain.

Only when he was in love did Mario Conde dare to think, mouth-wateringly, about the future. Switching on lights of hope for the future had become the most visible symptom of real amorous satisfaction, able to chase from his consciousness the nostalgia and melancholy he'd experienced in more than fifteen years of repeated failure. From the moment he had had to abandon university and shelve his literary aspirations, burying himself alive in an information bureau, classifying the horrors committed every day in the capital, in the country (types of crime, modus operandi, for hundreds of crimes and police reports), his paths in life had taken the most malevolent turnings: he'd married the wrong woman, his parents died within a year and Skinny Carlos came back from Angola in a wheelchair, with a broken back and languished like a tree stunted by bad pruning. Happiness and the joys of life had been trapped in a past that turned ever more utopian and out of reach, and only a propitious breath of love, in a fairytale, could restore them to his reality and life. Because, although in love with a remarkably lascivious redhead, Mario Conde knew his destiny was on course for the darkness of a lunar night: hopes of writing, feeling and behaving like a normal person with a stake in Lady Luck's capricious lottery were increasingly remote, because he also knew his life was linked to Skinny Carlos's fate – when Josefina left for ever he'd not allow his friend to waste away, sad and neglected, in a hospital for the disabled. Though he wasn't at all prepared, sooner or later he'd have to confront fear of the future which kept him awake and made breathing difficult. Solitude was like an endless tunnel because – and this was one of the many things he did know – no woman would agree to share with him that tougher test that destiny – destiny? – held in reserve.

193

Only when he fell in love did Mario Conde allow himself the luxury of forgetting that life sentence and feel a desire to write, dance and make love, to discover that the animal instincts released by the sexual act could also be a happy spur to give body and memory to life's dreams and forgotten promises. That was why, on that unique day in his amorous curriculum, he felt the desire to masturbate watching a naked woman blowing a viscous melody on a golden saxophone.

"Take your clothes off, please," he asks and Karina's winning and winsome smile accompanies the act of removing her blouse and trousers.

"All your clothes," he demands and when he sees her naked, he represses one by one his desires to embrace, kiss, at least touch her, and undresses, watching her all the time: he's surprised by the stillness of her skin, darkened only by her nipples and the hair around her sex, that's a more subtle red, and by the precise origins of her arms, breasts and legs, joined elastically to the whole. Her slightly withdrawn hips, good for birthing, are much more than a promise. Everything on his learning curve with this woman is a surprise.

He then undresses the saxophone and feels its cold firmness between his fingers for the first time, assessing the unexpected weight of an instrument embedded in his erotic fantasies that is about to become a most palpable reality.

"Sit here," he points her to the chair and gives her the sax. "Play something beautiful, please," he asks moving to another chair.

"What do you want to do?" she enquires, stroking the metal mouthpiece.

"Eat you," he says and repeats, "Play."

Karina is still fingering the mouthpiece and smiling hesitantly. She lifts it to her lips and sucks, dribbling saliva that hangs likes silver threads from her mouth. She makes her bum comfortable on the edge of the chair and opens her legs. She places the sax's long neck between her thighs and closes her eyes. A jagged, metallic lament begins to issue from the instrument's golden mouth and Mario Conde feels the melody pierce his chest, while Karina's serene figure – eyes shut, legs open towards fleshy, redder, darker depths, splitting her down the middle, breasts shaking to the music's rhythm and her breathing – take his desires to unimagined, unbearable peaks, while his eyes scour her every cranny and his two hands slowly run the length and mass of his penis, which begins to ooze drops of amber that make handling easier, and he closes in on her and her music to caress her neck and back, vertebra by vertebra, and her face – eyes, cheeks, forehead – with the purplish head of his member, as if erupting and leaving behind the wet trail of a wounded animal. She breathes in deeply and stops playing.

195

"Play," the Count insists, but his order comes out in a plaintive whisper and Karina exchanges cold metal for hot skin.

"Give me some of that," she asks and kisses his inflamed head, triangular in its latest incarnation, before her whole mouth sets out in search of a melody she can join . . . Tongues in thrall they walk to his bedroom and make love on the cleanest sheets, that smell of sun, soap and Lenten winds. They die, resurrect, only to die again . . .

He completed the ritual of foam creation and poured out the coffee. She had pulled on one of the sweaters the Count washed that afternoon and, when she sat down, it covered the top of her thighs. She wore the sandals made by Candito. He had wrapped a towel round his waist and pulled a chair over very close to hers.

"Are you going to stay the night?"

Karina tasted her coffee and looked at him.

"I don't think so. I've got a lot of work on tomorrow. I'd rather sleep at my place."

"So would I," he added not without irony.

"Mario, it's early days. Don't get too demanding."

He lit a cigarette and stopped himself from throwing the match in the sink. He stood up and looked for a metal ashtray.

"I get very jealous," he said trying to smile.

196

She asked him for a cigarette and puffed twice. He felt he was really jealous.

"Have you read the book yet?"

She nodded and finished her coffee.

"It depressed me, you know? But if you like it so much it's because you're a bit like one of Salinger's children. You like a tormented life."

"I don't really. It wasn't my choice. I didn't even choose you: something placed you in my path. When you're over thirty you learn to be resigned: you'll never do what you haven't yet done, and everything's a repeat. If you've triumphed, you'll have more triumphs; if you've failed, get used to the taste of failure. And I am used to it. But when something like you appears, you tend to forget all that, even the advice given out by Caridad Delgado."

Karina rubbed the palms of her hands over her thighs and tried to extend the scant cover given by the pullover.

"And what will happen if we can't go on together?"

The Count looked at her. He couldn't understand how, after so much loving, she could even imagine such a thing. Though he couldn't get the same thought out of his mind.

"I don't even want to think about that. I can't," he said but, "Karina . . . I think man's destiny is fulfilled by the quest, not by discovery, even though all finds seem to crown such efforts: the Golden Fleece, America, the theory of relativity . . . love. I prefer to search after the eternal. Not like Jason or Columbus, who died poor and disillusioned after so much searching. Rather a searcher after El Dorado, the impossible. I hope I never discover you, Karina, never find you on a tree, not even protected by a dragon, like the old Fleece. Don't ever let me catch you, Karina."

"It scares me to hear you talk like that," she said getting up. "You think too much." She picked up her saxophone that she'd abandoned on the floor and put it in its case. The Count looked at her bum, that the pullover no longer covered, small and red from the heat of the chair, and thought it didn't matter she had such a small butt. He was contemplating a myth not a woman, he told himself, as the telephone rang.

The Count looked at his clock on the night table and wondered who it could be at that hour.

"Yes," he said into the receiver.

"Conde, it's me, Cicerón. This business is getting murkier."

"What's happened, pal?"

"Lando the Russian. He turned up in Boca de Jaruco, by the riverbank. He was about to bid us all farewell from a motor launch when they caught him . . . How does the news strike you?"

The Count sighed. He felt the horizon was starting to lighten with a faint but unmistakable ray of sunlight.

"I'm delighted. When will you hand him over?" The silence at the other end of the line annoyed the detective lieutenant. "When? Cicerón?" he repeated.

"Is tomorrow morning OK?"

"Huh-huh, but don't hand him over in too drowsy a state," and he hung up.

When he got back to his living room he found a dressed and smiling Karina, her saxophone in its case, like a suitcase ready to depart.

"I'm off, Mr Policeman," she said and the Count felt a desire to tie her down. She's off, she's off. I'll always be searching for her.

"There he is then, Conde."

Captain Cicerón seemed more sleepy than happy when he pointed out the man scratching his chin on the other side of the translucent glass. An apt nickname: he really looked Russian. His fair, almost white, hair cascaded gently over his perfectly round head and ruddy vodka-drinker's face. In a high-collared jacket you might have mistaken him for Alyosha Karamazov, thought the Count, who'd had to move Manolo away from the glass to get a definitive view of his best lead. He noted the man's tired, bloodshot eyes and tried to find a path into that sombre look, to travel to necessary revelations, until he felt myopic exhaustion hit the bridge of his nose.

"And what did you get out of him?"

"He told me all about the clandestine escape they'd planned, but I've yet to extract anything about drugs. I'm still waiting on the laboratory analyses, the scrape from his fingers and, most spectacularly, the remains of a joint we found in the yard of the beach house where Lando and his cronies were staying."

"How many were there?"

"Four in the motor launch: Lando and his girlfriend and two other friends, Osvaldo Díaz and Roberto Navarro. They gave a kind of goodbye party on Saturday with lots of people. They invited everyone, down to the family cat. Incredible, don't you think?"

"What about the woman and the guys?"

"We've working on them too. They interest you?"

The Count shifted Manolo away from the glass again. Lando was now chewing his nails and spitting the bits out, with the weary mannerisms of your typical addict of marijuana and other evanescent flavours. Lissette and Lando? he wondered, at a loss for words. When he turned round he found Fabricio smirking next to Cicerón.

"See how we caught him, Conde?" he asked, and the Count couldn't decide whether the question was euphoric or heavily sarcastic.

"He couldn't ever escape from you," he replied opting to deflect back any sarcasm.

"No, he was never going to get away from me," Fabricio agreed.

"Well then," interjected Cicerón, "what's your next step, Conde?"

"Let me start hereabouts. I have a hunch . . ."

"A hunch?" asked Manolo smiling. The Count looked into his eyes and the sergeant glanced back at the detainee.

"But first I need the results from the laboratory. You wait there, Lando," he said, gesturing towards the glass. For his part, Lando had stopped biting his nails and was leaning his head on the edge of the table. You're ripe for the picking, thought the Count and went into the passageway, brushing his shoulder against the arm of Lieutenant Fabricio who didn't move aside to make way for him. This guy is asking for it, the Count muttered.

Lando looked up when he heard the door. It was a slow, rusty sound like the look in his brown eyes. The Count glanced at him and walked over to the back wall, as Manolo dropped a folder full of papers on the table. The lieutenant lit a cigarette and observed his colleague's idiosyncratic habits. Manolo had seated himself on one corner of the table, perching one lean buttock on the wood, and swinging the foot that didn't reach the floor. He opened the folder and started to read as if enthralled. He occasionally looked up at Lando, as if his face might serve as an illustration of what he was

201

reading. For his part, the Russian shifted his gaze from the folder to the sergeant's eyes.

Although the laboratory had confirmed the similar origins of the marijuana belonging to Lando and Lissette, a large measure of Conde's hunch was discounted by the analysts' verdict: Orlando San Juan's blood was B negative and his fingerprints didn't match any found in Lissette's flat. For a moment he'd thought Lando's clandestine flight might be from a murder rap. The Count now clung to the remote possibility of a relationship between that character and the deceased chemistry teacher. And Casino Deportivo? Caridad Delgado? The headmaster? he wondered, keen to put those questions. The case's immediate fate depended on this interrogation and the two policemen knew the value of the card they were playing.

Manolo finally shut the file and put it down almost within reach of the detainee. He stood up and went to sit in the armchair, the other side of the table, away from the torrid lamps of the interrogation cubicle.

"Well, Major," he said keeping his eyes trained on Lando, "this is Orlando San Juan Grenet. He was arrested last night trying to desert the country in a stolen motor launch and he's additionally held on drugs and murder charges."

Lando's eyes suddenly woke up.

"What was that? Who've I murdered? You mad or what?"

202

Manolo smiled pleasantly.

"Don't ever speak again unless spoken to. And don't ever call me mad again, get that?"

"But the fact is . . ."

"But the fact is you can shut up!" shouted Manolo, standing up, and even Conde looked startled in his corner. He'd never been able to understand where his colleague found his brute, heavyweight strength. "As I was saying, Major, we found the remains of a marijuana joint in the house the detainee rented in Guanabo, marijuana from Central America, and two people arrested for possession of that drug have identified Orlando San Juan as their supplier. This is most serious, as you appreciate. But that isn't all, the very same drug was found in the flat of a young woman who was murdered a week ago and we'll try the detainee for that crime as well."

Lando started to gesture as if in protest, but said nothing. He shook his head, as if he couldn't credit his ears. The Count leaned forward off the wall and crushed his cigarette on the floor. He took a step towards the table and looked at Lando.

"Orlando, you're in a dicey situation, you know?"

"But I know nothing about any dead woman."

"Didn't you know Lissette Núñez Delgado?"

"Lissette? No, I know a Lissette who left sometime ago. She landed an Italian and found herself a better life. She lives in Milan now."

"But a joint made from the marijuana you've been peddling was found in the house of the Lissette I'm referring to."

"Look, general, I'm sorry but I don't know that woman and haven't been peddling anything, I swear . . . Do you want me to swear an oath?"

"No, that won't be necessary, Orlando, it's easy to prove. An identity parade with the two dealers we've pulled in can do the trick. They'll identify you because they're dying to get a few years knocked off their sentence. Tell me something, did you sell marijuana to anyone involved in La Víbora Pre-Uni?"

"At Pre-Uni? No, I've never been involved with that place . . ."

"Then tell me about Caridad Delgado."

"Never heard of her."

Conde found another cigarette in his pocket and lit up slowly. Lando the Russian wasn't going to admit to his connection with drugs, especially if he'd had any kind of relationship with Lissette. But he went on, chasing his only tangible lead: "Orlando, this isn't the first time you've had problems with us and we really don't like seeing the same faces returning, you get me? We don't like you giving us so much to do. But at the end of the day we do our homework. You'll be here until we know the hour your great-great-grandfather was born and the rest, because you'll tell us. Now tell us what you know about Lissette Núñez, and the marijuana that ended up at her place or should we meet again at twelve after the late-night film?"

Lando the Russian scratched his chin again, shaking his head. His eyes had darkened another degree and his look was despairingly opaque.

"I swear to you, general, I know nothing about any of that," he said and shook his head again. At that moment the Count would have given anything to know what lay under the apocryphal Russian's crop of fair hair that danced to the endless shaking of his head.

"Come on, Manolo. See you later, Orlando, and thanks for the promotion to general."

La vie en rose, sang Bola de Nieve, taking a chance with his French and openly challenging Edith Piaf. Terrific, the Count muttered and tried to think for a moment: interrogation cubicles provoke a feeling of enclosure that nurtures confessions. They are the anteroom to trial and prison, and finding yourself defenceless there can be a burden that's hard to bear. To leave those four cold, oppressive walls is like a resurrection. But the presence of a policeman in an everyday environment can trigger the unexpected: fear and suspicion spring up with the need to conceal that undesirable apparition from others, and sometimes such fears cause the hare to make the necessary leap. Tra-la-la, he hummed. No

205

stopping this policeman: and he decided he'd go and see the head teacher on home territory. He'd go back to Pre-Uni. A very vague idea had come to him while talking to Lando, and he'd suggested to Manolo they should go and converse with the head.

It was a benign Monday morning outside headquarters. The wind had declared a truce and a resolutely summery sun varnished the city streets. Manolo had tuned into a programme dedicated to Bola de Nieve on the radio and the Count decided to concentrate on the voice and piano of the man who *was* the song he sang: he was singing 'La Flor de la Canela', 'with jasmine in her hair and roses on her face . . .' and the lieutenant remembered the unexpected end to his last meeting with Karina. He saw himself disarmed, without arguments to prevent her departure, when she was dressed and saying goodbye on his doorstep and, looking more like a whinging kid than a pursuer of myths, he felt like stamping the ground. Why was she leaving him? The wholehearted surrender of that woman transformed by the sharp scent of sex didn't fit with the unbridgeable distance she'd then imposed. From the start he'd thought he should have talked more, got to know and understand her, but what with his desperate monologues and the sexual conflagrations that absorbed them, there'd hardly been time to breathe, recharge batteries and drink a coffee.

The car drove very close to the hospital where Jorrín lay and turned into Santa Catalina, an avenue planted with flamboyant trees and memories, parties, cinemas and emotional discoveries of every kind, a *vie en rose* that seemed increasingly remote in his memory, locked in a time that was lost for ever, like paradise itself. Bola de Nieve was now singing *Duerme, negrito* and the Count wondered: how can he sing like that? It was a melodious whisper exploring subdued, daring notes, rarely visited because of the narrowness of that final frontier between song and mere murmur. The flamboyant trees on Santa Catalina had resisted the battering from the winds, their red flowery crests a challenge to any artist. Outside the walls of headquarters life sometimes seemed normal, almost *en rose*.

Manolo parked to one side of Pre-Uni and switched off the radio. He yawned and his over-prominent bones shook, as he asked: "Well, where are we at?"

"The head hasn't told us everything he knows."

"Who ever does, Conde?"

"It's a very peculiar case, Manolo: everybody's lying, I don't know if it's to protect someone or protect themselves or because it's a habit they can't give up. I'm up to here with all this lying. But what I'm after now is what this man can tell us."

"Do you think it was him?"

"I don't know, I don't know anything, but I do think he doesn't . . ."

207

"What then?"

The Count looked at the school's sturdy structure. He was now wondering whether he hadn't decided to see the head simply because he wanted to return, as if eternally guilty, to the scene of his favourite crimes.

"There's a third man in this story, Manolo. I lay my neck on it. The first one is Pupy, who's got a lot of fingers in the pie but I don't think he'd have dared, he's got too much street sense to ruin it with a woman whose antics he was too familiar with. Besides, he knew how to get what he wanted from her. He'd never have strayed so far. The second is the head teacher, who has even got good reason: he was in love and probably jealous. But if his alibi stands, it would have been impossible for him to go to Lissette's at eleven, and batter and kill her. And the third man? If there is a third, he was the one who killed her and he must have been at the party, and although Lando's fingerprints didn't show up in the flat, I've not yet ruled him out. This is how I see things right now: the party ended, the third man stayed behind and for some reason killed Lissette, because of something she did to him or refused to give him. Because he didn't stay to rob or rape her – neither of those things happened – and it's even possible the last one to bed her didn't murder her. What did Lissette have to interest him? Drugs? Information?"

"Information," replied Manolo. His eyes glinted with joy.

"Huh-huh. Information about what? About drugs?"

"No, I don't think so. She was always a live wire but I don't think she was part of Lando's set up and was always careful not to burn her fingers."

"But, just think, Caridad Delgado only lives three blocks away from Lando."

"You think they knew each other?"

"I really don't know. But what information could she have had?"

"She knew something."

"Or rather something worth money, right?"

Manolo nodded and looked at the Pre-Uni.

"What's the headmaster got to do with all this?"

"I don't know whether it's straightforward . . . or convoluted. But I think he knows the third man we're after."

"Hey, Conde, this is like the Orson Welles film they showed the other day."

"Don't tell me you watched a film? Great! One of these days you'll be telling me you've read a book . . ."

"Today I am in a position to offer you a cup of tea," said the headmaster pointing them to the sofa that occupied one wall of his office.

"No, thanks," said the Count.

"I don't want any either," added Manolo.

The head shook his head, as if disappointed, and

pulled his chair up until it was opposite the policemen. He seemed prepared for a long exchange and the Count thought perhaps he'd chosen badly again.

"Well, have you got anywhere?"

The Count lit up and regretted not accepting the tea. The only coffee he'd drunk at dawn had left a feeling of abandon in an empty stomach he'd neglected after wolfing the leftovers of the chicken rice that had survived Skinny Carlos's hunger. A hungry cop isn't a good one, he thought and said: "The investigation is ongoing and I must remind you you're still on the list of suspects. You're one of the five people who might have been in Lissette's house the night she was killed, and you had good reason to kill her, despite your alibi."

The headmaster shifted uneasily, as if startled by an alarm bell. He looked round, as if worrying about the privacy of his office.

"But why do you say that, lieutenant? Isn't what my wife told you enough?" His tone was pitiful, a barely contained anguish, and the Count thought again: no, he was in the right place.

"For the moment let's just say we believe her, headmaster, and don't worry. We're not interested in messing up your marriage and quiet family life, let alone your prestige in this school, after twenty years in post, I can assure you of that. Is it fifteen or twenty?"

"So what do you want, then?" he asked, ignoring the exact figure the Count was after, hands raised like a child expecting to be punished.

"Apart from Pupy and you, what other man was having an affair with Lissette?"

"No, but she . . ."

"Look, headmaster, please don't lie to us, because this is a serious matter, and I can't stand any more lies from you, or anyone else. Can I remind you of a little detail? She went to bed with Pupy so he'd give her presents. Did you ever look in her wardrobe? I imagine you did and you saw how full it was, I expect? Shall I remind you of another little detail? She went to bed with you because that gave her impunity here in Pre-Uni to do what she wanted. And don't contradict me again, right?"

The headmaster made a weary attempt at a protest, but thought better of it. Seemingly, as he'd said on the last occasion, those policemen knew everything. Everything?

"Look at this photo," and the Count handed him the card with Orlando San Juan's image.

"No, I don't know him. Are you going to tell me he was another of Lissette's men?"

Of course I'd obviously spoken to Lissette several times about all this. I could understand how a woman like her, so young, so pretty, and revolutionary – well, I think she was a revolutionary – would want to live like that, be with other people in the way she was with me, as if I didn't count . . . She was very mixed up. I'm getting on now, what could I give her? It's clear enough: impunity at work, like Pupy gave her jeans or perfume, OK? True enough, it's sordid and shameful . . . I looked at her and couldn't believe my eyes: she had spirit, enviable amounts of the stuff. Where did she get it from? Maybe her upbringing. Her mother and father were too busy with their own business and tried to compensate the time they couldn't give her by showering her with clothes and other privileges. She was always by herself and learned to live for herself. And what they bred was a Frankenstein. But the fact is one never learns: I've been twenty-six years in this job – not fifteen or twenty – and I know what goes into these dolls, because they start to grow up here. I've seen so many! They're the ones who always say, "Yes, why not?" and are up for whatever and never argue, and everyone says, look at that, what a great attitude – although they don't then care whether or not they do things, let alone whether they do them well. What stays on the retina is this: they're flexible, timely, always at the ready, and, naturally, they'll never argue, think or create problems . . . And then we too say they are good, blue-eyed boys and girls, plus all the other things people say. That's what went into Lissette, though she did think and did know what she wanted.

And I'm such a shit-bag I even fell in love with her . . .
It's hardly surprising if the girl made me feel what I'd
never ever felt, took me where I'd never been taken
before. Of course I was going to fall in love with her,
you must understand that . . . Although I started to find
things out that were scary, but as I told myself, this won't
last, let's live it while I can. Yes, she had an affair with
one pupil, if not more, I'm not sure. No, I don't know
who it is, but I'm almost sure it was someone she taught.
Course I didn't dare ask her, after all, what right had I
to tell her what to do? I found out about a month ago,
when I came across one of those olive-green – military
style – backpacks that youths like today, you know the
ones I mean? It was next to her bed. I asked, "What's
this, Lissette?" She made nothing of it, said a pupil
had left it behind in the classroom, but she was clearly
lying, if she'd have found one, she'd have left it with the
secretary, wouldn't she? But I asked no more questions.
I didn't want to. And couldn't. And the day she was
killed, there was a uniform shirt in her bathroom. It
was hanging up wet. When I left, it was still there. But
I don't think a young kid can have done what they did
to her. I really don't. I told you they can be apathetic,
lazy when it comes to studying, wasters, as they say, but
they'd never go that far. But I've committed no crime,
nobody can sit in judgement on me because of what I
did, I fell in love like a young boy, worse, like an old'un,

and I'd give my right arm for nothing to have happened to Lissette. You're policemen, but men as well, you must understand all this?

The Count surveyed the playground where the numbered posts for lining up classes still stood like remnants of an obsolete order. In his time the line at the back was the favourite, the furthest away from the headmaster and his retinue of speechmakers and persecutors of moustaches, sideburns and hair over the ears. Years later, that passion long spent, the Count was still upset by the constant repression they'd suffered simply because they were young and wanted to act as such. Perhaps Skinny, with his redemptive sense of memory, might say of all that, "But, Conde, for hell's sake, who remembers any of that?" He'd forgotten other things, but couldn't forgive that perverse assault on what any youngster wanted to do at that age: let his hair grow, feel it rest on his ears, curl round his shirt collar, be able to show it off at Saturday night parties and compete in being way out, as they all said, with the kids who'd left school and wore their hair how they liked . . . When he got to university and nobody asked him to crop it, the Count adopted remorselessly the hairstyle he still maintained: longish hair all round. But the memory of lining up at 1 p.m. almost made him break out in a sweat.

"Manolo, don't kick up a fuss in there but I need a list of all Lissette's male pupils, the ones she had this year

214

and last, and the marks they all got for chemistry. And look out for the name of José Luis Ferrer. Look for all his marks you can find. Got that?"

"Can you repeat that?" asked the sergeant, looking like a rather droopy schoolboy.

"Go to hell, Manolo, and don't ask for a tongue-lashing. You went too far this morning with Cicerón and Fabricio, so just calm down . . . I'm going to her place again, the shirt's probably still there and we missed it. When you're finished here, pick me up, clear?"

"Clear as water, Conde."

The lieutenant left the foyer in the administration wing without saying goodbye to a defeated, almost pathetic headmaster. He walked down one of the long side corridors and turned to the right and walked to the end. Halfway down one passage he looked out over the parapet and found it had hardly changed: he put one leg over the wall, dropped on to an eave and, as he'd done day after day for a year, scrambled down the wall bars to get into the PE yard. As ever, freedom and the street were but one step away. And the Count ran as if the very fate of the bold Guaytabó was at stake in his mortal struggle against Anatolio, the cunning Turk, or Supanqui, the fearsome Indian. Then he heard someone whistle.

The author of that summons had followed in his footsteps, jumped over the wall, shinned down the bars and now ran over to him.

"I saw you through the window and asked to be allowed to go to the lavatory," announced José Luis and his rickety, chain-smoker's chest shook from the effort and his coughing.

"Let's go into the street," suggested the Count and they walked towards the laurels growing at the back of Pre-Uni. "How are you?" he asked offering him a cigarette.

"Fine, fine," he said, but he was nervous and looked back twice at the building he'd just left.

"You'd rather we left here?"

The youth thought for a second and said: "Yes, let's sit down round the corner."

"Skinny and me," thought the Count and he chose the wall of the liquor shop where Skinny and he used to sit after their PE lessons.

"Well, what happened?"

José Luis threw his cigarette at the street and rubbed his hands as if he were cold.

"Nothing really, lieutenant, I've been thinking about the mess you told me about the other day and the fact that someone's dead and I started to think . . ."

"And?"

"Nothing, lieutenant, I've . . ." he repeated himself and looked back at Pre-Uni. "Things happen you probably don't know about. There are many people here up to their necks in it, and the trick is to keep your head down

216

and not get into trouble. That's why everybody will tell you Lissette the teacher was real nice."

"I don't get you, José Luis."

The boy forced a smile.

"Don't make it difficult for me, lieutenant, it's not easy saying this: she used to pass everyone . . . She'd do revisions two or three days before the exam and would include the same exercises that would be in the exams. You get me? Well, she'd change a percentage here, an element or formula there, but it was basically the same and the whole class went crazy and got top marks."

"Do lots of people know about this? Didn't anyone ever tell the headmaster, for example?"

"I don't know, lieutenant. I think a young girl may have mentioned it in a Young Communist meeting, but as I don't belong . . . I don't know if they talked about it anywhere else."

"And what else did she do?"

"Well, things other teachers didn't do. She'd go to parties with people from her class, or from the barrio, and dance with us and lay the odd one, well, you know . . ."

"Well, she wasn't much older than you people."

"Yes, that's true. But sometimes she'd go one clinch too far. And she was a teacher, wasn't she?"

The Count looked at the fragment of Pre-Uni you could see through the foliage. Going to bed with a teacher had always been the number one dream of the pupils who'd passed through its portals over fifty years; even he'd dreamed about his literature teacher and told himself she was Cortázar's *Maga*. He looked at José Luis: it would be too much to ask, he thought, but he asked anyway: "Which pupil was going to bed with her?"

José Luis turned his head, as if caught in a sudden draught. Rubbed his hands together again and swung his foot to and fro.

"I don't know, lieutenant."

The Count placed his hand on his thigh and stopped his leg from swinging.

"Yes, you do, José Luis, and you're going to tell me."

"I really don't, lieutenant," the skinny youth protested and tried to sound sure of himself again, "I wasn't one of her little gang."

"Look," said the Count taking his battered notebook out of his back pocket. "Let's do one thing. Trust me: nobody will ever know we talked about this. Ever. Write down the names of her little gang. Do me this favour, José Luis, because if one of them had anything to do with Lissette's death and you don't help me, you'll never forgive yourself later on. Help me," the Count repeated, as he handed the youth his notebook and pen. José Luis shook his head, as if to say, "Why the fuck did I ever leave that classroom?"

* * *

If they were the last act of the Creation, after six days in which God experimented in every imaginable way and created out of nothing heaven and earth, plants and animals, rivers and woods, and even man himself, that wretch Adam, women must be the most perfect, most considered invention in the universe, starting with Eve herself, who had showed herself to be much wiser and able than Adam. That's why they have all the questions and all the answers, and I'm just one truth and one doubt: I'm in love, but, but with a woman I can't get to know. Really, Karina, who are you?

The Count peered over the balcony and gazed at the restless contours of Santos Suárez, focussing on the spot on the horizon where he'd located Karina's house. The need to penetrate that woman via the hitherto inviolable keyhole of her hidden history now became an obsession calling on the best impulses of his intellect. He returned his notebook to his pocket because he again felt the oppressive presence of that torrid wind on the fourth floor that wouldn't agree to leave the last flowers of spring or Mario Conde's perennial melancholy in peace.

Under the aggressive midday sun the roof terraces were like red deserts, off-limits to human life. One floor lower, opposite, the Count sought out the window that made him a peeping tom to a matrimonial drama and found

219

it open, as on that first day, but the scene had changed: behind a sewing machine, taking advantage of the bright light streaming in, the woman was hard at work and listening to the chatter of the man who was rocking in his chair. They now performed a rather classic, recherché domestic drama that included the action of drinking coffee from the same cup. End of soap, thought Conde as he shut his balcony window and switched off the lights in the flat. For a moment he tried again to imagine what happened six days ago and realized it must have been something horrific: as if a ruthless Lent storm had let rip there before tyrannizing the city. Standing up in the half-dark, opposite the chalk profile on the tiles, the Count saw the back of a man striking a woman, gripping her neck and squeezing it tight. He only needed to touch the white shirt on the shoulder to see a face – one of three possible faces, all three strangers to him – and end that business he now thought most pathetic.

He went down to wait for Manolo, but stopped off on the third floor. He knocked on the door of the flat underneath Lissette's and after his second knock confronted a face he felt was remotely familiar: an old man he calculated was in his eighties, with his scant wisps of grey hair and elephant ears about to take flight, was peering at him through the half-open door.

"Good day," said Conde, taking his police credentials out of his pocket. "It's to do with the girl in the top flat," he explained to the corrugated cardboard ear the old man presented, which nodded affirmatively when its owner seemed about to open the door.

"Take a seat," the old man suggested and the Count entered a space similar but different to the one he'd just left. The old man's living-room was full of solid, antique mahogany and wickerwork furniture that matched the glass cabinet and centre table. But everything appeared to be recently turned and polished by a master carpenter.

"Beautiful furniture," conceded the Count.

"I made them, almost fifty years ago. And I keep them like this," he said, really proudly. "The secret is to clean the dust off with water and alcohol, and not to use the solutions they sell these days to bring out the shine."

"It's good to make things like this, isn't it? That are beautiful and lasting."

"What?" the old man whimpered, who'd forgotten to re-orientate his hearing aids.

"They are very beautiful," said the Count raising his voice several decibels.

"And they're not the best I made, by a long way. Do you remember the Gómez Menas, the millionaires? I made them a library and dining room of genuine African ebony. That was what you called wood: hard, but elegant to fashion. God knows where that landed up when they all left."

"Someone's got them, don't you worry."

"No, I don't worry. For hell's sake, at my age I'm

immunized against practically everything and rarely worry. Pissing properly is my biggest concern in life, can you credit that?"

The Count smiled and, seeing an ashtray on the coffee table, ventured to take out a cigarette.

"You're a Canary islander, aren't you?"

The old man's smile bared teeth ravaged by history.

"From La Palma, the Pretty Isle. Why do you ask?"

"My Granddad was from there and you're like him."

"Then we're almost fellow countrymen. Come on, what can I do for you?"

"Look, the day it happened upstairs," said the Count, who thought it inappropriate to mention the word death here, where it seemed nigh, "there was a party or something similar. Music and booze. Did you see anyone go upstairs?"

"No, I just heard the din."

"Was anyone here with you?"

"My wife, who's just gone out on a few errands, but the poor dear is deafer than me and heard nothing . . . When she removes her gadget . . . And my children don't live here anymore. They've lived in Madrid for the past twenty years."

"But you've seen some of the people who visit Lissette, haven't you?"

"Yes, a few. But there were lots, you know? Particularly young lads. Not very many women, you know?"

"Lads in school uniform?"

The Old Man smiled, as did the Count, because he saw in his half smile the cheekiness his Granddad Rufino adopted when talking to women who told him they were divorced. That kind of smile had the Count believing for many a year that divorcées were whores.

"Yes, a goodly number."

"And could you identify any if you had to?"

The old man hesitated. And finally shook his head.

"I don't think so: when you're twenty everybody looks alike . . . And the same goes at eighty. But let me tell you something, my compatriot, something I decided not to tell the others, but as I like you . . ." He paused to swallow and held out a hand of strong fingers whose joints were like badly tied knots. "That girl was a bad piece of work, and that's from me, a man who's seen two wars in his lifetime. It's not surprising she had this bother. Once they were jumping up and down in one of their parties as if they'd gone mad, and I thought the ceiling would crash down on us. I don't like interfering in other's people's lives, ask around, if you like . . . because I won't let anyone interfere in mine. But that day I had no choice but to go up and tell them to stop jumping so much. And do you know what she said: she said I should be ashamed to protest . . . that I should clear off with my lousy children, because I was the father of lousy kids who'd left the island and more besides, and that she'd do what she wanted in her house. Obviously she was drunk, and she could say that because she was a woman, because if a man had said that to me I'd have been the one who'd have killed her . . . OK, I've done it, now, right? And if I'm going to be in pain when I'm pissing, prison or Central Park, it's all the same. She was bad, my compatriot, and people like that can make any man flip. That's all I have to . . . Look, I'm a shitty old man who can hardly even speak and even the food I eat hurts me, and I'm living on borrowed time. But I'm glad it happened to her, and say as much quite without remorse and without expecting God's forgiveness, because I've known that dickhead's not existed for quite some time. What do you reckon?"

"Conde, Conde, Conde," Manolo jumped up and down as happy as a birthday boy, when the lieutenant came out of the building. "I think we've got it," he said, pointing at his closed fist.

"What happened, then?" asked Conde trying not to seem too enthused. In truth, the conversation with the old carpenter had depressed him: it must be terrible to live thinking about the pain from your next pee. But he liked the mixture of love and hate still bubbling up in that lunatic on the edge of the grave.

"Look, Conde, if what I found on the Pre-Uni lists checks out, then we're all done here."

"But what did you find, pal?"

"Listen to this. I made a list one by one of the names of Lissette's pupils, beginning with this year's lot, and then went on to the previous lot, who are now in their last year. I came across José Luis, who got ninety-seven in chemistry, and ninety-two in everything else. I reckon he's a top student, don't you? You know, I was getting fed up of listing names and marks and it left me cold until I reached the last name on the last list from last year. You do know that the lists are alphabetical, don't you?"

The Count wiped his hand over his face. Do I hang or behead him? he pondered.

"Get to the point, guy."

"Hell, Conde, keep your hair on, the best about all this is the suspense. It was just what I found. You write down name after name and finally, when there's only one pupil left, you get to the name that can get us to the bottom of this pile of shit."

"Lázaro San Juan Valdés."

The sergeant's surprise was spectacular: he raised his arms as if a dog had bitten him, dropping all the papers, like a crestfallen child.

"Hell, Conde, you knew all along?"

"A little bird whispered in my ear when I left Pre-Uni," smiled the Count, showing him the sheet of paper that bore three names: Lázaro San Juan Valdés, Luis Gustavo Rodríguez and Yuri Samper Oliva. "Yes, San Juan, as in

Orlando San Juan, alias Lando the Russian. Hey, Manolo, how many San Juans are there in Havana?"

"Fuck his mother's cunt, Conde, it's got to be him," replied Manolo, as he ran after the list of names the wind was blowing away.

"Off we go to headquarters, then. And put your foot down if you want, because you've got leave today," he said, although he had to withdraw his authorization six blocks on.

"Hey, Conde, I'm really hungry."

"And do I live on air?"

"Don't force me to go upstairs now," begged Manolo when they walked into headquarters.

"Go on then, get something to eat and tell them to keep something back for me even if it's only bread. I'm going up."

Sergeant Manuel Palacios went down the passage to the canteen, as his chief pressed the lift button. The figures, on the board, showed it was on its way down but Conde kept his finger on the button until the doors opened and then pressed for the fourth floor. In the corridor he decided to make a pit stop in the lavatory. He'd not urinated since he'd got up, almost six hours ago, and he anxiously watched a spurt of dark, fetid pee hit the bowl and raise reddish foam. My kidneys are fucked, he thought, as he hurriedly shook himself. That

226

must be why I'm losing weight, and he remembered the old carpenter and his wee worries.

He returned to the corridor and pushed on the door to the Drugs Department. The main room was empty and the Count was afraid Captain Cicerón was out on the street, but he rapped the glass in his office door.

"Come in," he heard and turned the door handle.

Lieutenant Fabricio was sitting in one of the office chairs nearest to the desk. The Count looked at him and his first thought was to leave but he stopped himself: he had no reason to beat a retreat and decided to be pleasant, like any well-bred citizen. Hang on, he thought.

"Good afternoon?"

"What was that?" came the reply.

"Where's the captain?"

"I don't know," came the reply, as Fabricio put the papers he was reading down on the desk, "I think he's having lunch."

"You think or don't know?" asked the Count, making an effort not to seem supercilious.

"Why do you need to see him?" asked Fabricio, slowing the pace of the exchange.

"Please, tell me where he is, it's urgent."

Fabricio smiled and asked: "And can't you tell me what's it's about? If it's concerning Lando, I should say I'm in charge of that case now."

"Well, congratulations."

"Hey, Conde, you know I don't like your sarcasm or your arrogance," said Fabricio, standing up.

The Count thought he should count to ten but didn't bother. There were witnesses and it might be a good opportunity to help Fabricio sort out once and for all his problems of taste in matters of sarcasm and arrogance. Even though they kick me out of headquarters, the force, the province and even the country.

"Hey, *chico*," the Count replied, "why the fuck do you keep needling me? You fancy me? Why keep coming on to me?"

Fabricio took one step forward to deliver his riposte.

"Hey, Conde, you go fuck yourself. Do you think this is your department as well?"

"Look, Fabricio, it's not mine and it's not yours, and I piss on your mother's twat," and he took a step forward, just as the door opened. The Count looked round and saw the figure of Captain Cicerón in the doorway.

"And what's going on here?" he asked.

The Count felt every muscle in his body was shaking and was afraid his rage would bring on tears. A sudden stabbing headache had started at the nape of his neck and spread to his forehead. He looked at Fabricio and his eyes promised all the shit they could.

"I needed to see you, Cicerón," the Count said finally, taking the Captain by the arm and leading him out of his office.

"What was going on back there, Conde?"

"Let's go into the corridor," asked the lieutenant. "I don't know what that bastard has got against me, but I'll not stand anymore. I swear I'll smash the bloody queer to pieces."

"Hey, calm down. What's got into you? You gone mad or what?"

His headache throbbed and throbbed, but Conde managed a smile.

"Forget it, Cicerón. Wait a minute," and he looked for an analgesic in his pocket. He went over to the tap and sluiced it down. He then extracted the pot of Chinese pomade from his other pocket and rubbed some over his forehead.

"You feeling ill?"

"Just a little headache. But it'll go. Hey, what's the news on Lando the Russian?"

Cicerón leaned against the big window in the corridor and took out his cigarettes. He offered the Count one and saw the lieutenant's hands were trembling. He shook his head.

"He's started to sing. We did a parade with the Luyanó people and they picked him out as the man who sold them marijuana in Vedado. He admitted as much and gave the names of two other buyers. But he says he bought the marijuana from a peasant from Escambray. I think he's invented someone but we're checking it out anyway."

"Look, in terms of the teacher, I've got a name that may have to do with Lando: Lázaro San Juan, a student at Pre-Uni."

Cicerón looked at his cigarette and thought for a moment.

"So you'd like to speak to him?"

"Huh-huh," the Count nodded and rubbed in more Chinese pomade. The searing heat from the balsam started to lighten the weight in his head.

"Come on, before it gets too late."

Cicerón opened the cubicle door and called the guards.

"You can take him now," he said as he positioned himself next to Conde to watch Lando the Russian leave. The ruddiness had faded from a face now pale with fear. He knew the noose was tightening and the unexpected questions about Lázaro San Juan had helped undermine his story.

"He's almost there, Cicerón," said Conde lighting the cigarette he'd postponed until after the interrogation.

"Let him stew a bit longer. I'll bring him back up in a minute. What are you going to do now?"

"I want to talk to the Boss. The fact Lázaro is Lando's nephew may hit Pre-Uni like a bombshell and I want him to tell me again I've got carte blanche to take it wherever it takes me. Shit may rain over La Víbora. Are you coming with me?"

230

"Yeah, let's see what this turns up. Hey, Conde, if Lando is covering up for someone it must be because it's someone important."

"So you think a mafia exists as well?"

"Who else does?"

"A friend of mine . . ."

Cicerón thought before he replied.

"If a mafia is a group of people organized to do the business, well, yes, I do."

"A local Creole mafia of marijuana dealers and such like? You're kidding, Cicerón. Can you imagine them and their molls eating spaghetti *à la napolitaine* here in Cuba, in 1989, with what a drop of tomato sauce costs you today?"

"No, I'm not kidding, because they're into big money and that drug didn't come from Escambray or wash up in some cove. This came straight into the hands of people who spread it around. There's a big organization behind this, I bet you whatever you like."

The corridors and staircases were a labyrinth that irritated a Count in a hurry. At every point you opened a door only to meet another. The last one led to the top, the highest in headquarters, where Maruchi was talking on the phone behind her desk.

"Cutie, I need to see top dog," said Conde leaning his knuckles on her desk.

"He went out about an hour ago, Mario."

231

Conde humphed and looked at Cicerón. The reply was too long in coming for the anxious lieutenant.

"But, my dear . . ." began Conde only to be interrupted.

"So you've not heard the news?" she asked and the Count stiffened. Alarm bells began to ring.

"What news?"

"It's downstairs on the noticeboard . . . Captain Jorrín died. At around eleven this morning. He had a massive heart attack. Major Rangel's gone over there."

"I was playing in the yard. God knows why I wasn't out with Granddad Rufino, or on the street corner playing basketball with other rascals or having a nap which is what my mother wanted. Look how skinny you are, she exclaimed, you've got worms, I bet. And I was *at that very moment* in the yard, *in fact* digging out earthworms to throw to the fighting cocks who pecked them up, when old Amérida ran *right* down the passage in her place that led into our yard shouting at the top of her voice: 'They've killed Kennedy, they've killed that bastard'. I've had a notion of death ever since, and especially of its unbearable mystery. I think that's why the priest in the barrio church didn't protest when I abandoned religion for baseball because of my doubts about his mystical explanation of the frontiers of death: faith didn't suffice for me to accept the existence of an eternal world with layers of the good in heaven, the not-so-bad in purgatory, the real baddies in hell and the innocent abroad in limbo forever – not as a theoretical account of what nobody had lived to tell, despite the fact I did make allowances when I was able to conjure the soul up as a transparent bag, full of reddish, murky gas, hanging off the ribs, next to the heart and ready to float away like a fugitive balloon at the moment of death. Only from that point was I convinced of the inevitability of death and, in particular, of its enduring presence and the real emptiness its arrival leaves: there is nothing, it is nothing, and that's why so many folk throughout the world console themselves one way or another by attempting to imagine something beyond nothingness, because the mere idea that man's time on earth is a brief interlude between two voids has been humanity's greatest source of anguish since it became conscious of its existence. That's why I can't get accustomed to death and it always surprises and terrifies me: it's a warning mine is closer, that the deaths of my dearest loved ones are nigh and that everything I've dreamed and lived, loved and hated, will also evaporate into nothingness. Who was he, what did he do, what did he think, that grandfather of my great-great-grandfather, of whom no name or trace remains? What will my potential great-great-grandson be, do, think at the end of the twenty-first century – if I ever get to procreate the one who should be his great-grandfather? It is horrific not to know the past and yet be able to impact on the future: that great-great-grandson will only exist if I start the chain, as I came into existence because that grandfather of my great-great-grandfather added to a chain tying him to the first monkey with a human face that put his feet into – onto – the earth. Hamlet and I with that same skull: no matter he's called Yorik and was a jester, or Jorrín and was a police captain, or Lissette Núñez and was a happy hooker at the end of the twentieth century. No matter."

"What are you doing, Conde? Come on, give me a cigarette." Manolo took the cigarette while he looked at the park where a group of kids had assembled who'd just left school for the day. Their white shirts formed a low, hyperkinetic cloud, caught between the benches and trees. Boys just like them, remembered the Count, so near and so far to the solemnity of death.

"I'm going to wait for the Boss to come out so I can talk to him."

An unmistakable odour that made Conde feel sick drifted over from the undertakers. He'd gone in for a second and seen the grey box containing Jorrín between flowers and family. Manolo had peered over the edge of the coffin to look at his face, but the Count kept his distance: it was disturbing enough to think that he'd remember Jorrín in his hospital bed, pallid and dozy without the eschatological extra of seeing him definitively dead. Too many dead. To hell with all this, Conde had told himself, refusing to offer his condolences to the family, as he sought out fresh air on the street and a vision of life. He'd like to have been far from there, beyond the grasp and memory of that absurd, melodramatic rite, but he decided to mount guard and wait for the Major.

"So how long do we have to put up with this bloody wind? I can't stand it any more," the Count protested, as an old man, carrying a pint of coffee, walked down the steps and over to the two policemen. He kept moving his mouth, as if chewing something light but indestructible, while his cheeks pumped air or saliva at a monotonous, regular rhythm, towards the engine that kept him on his feet. He wore a jacket that had seen too many autumns and black trousers stained by drops of piss he'd splashed around his fly.

"Give me a cigarette, amigo?" the old man asked quietly, and gestured as if to receive the smoke he'd requested.

The Count, who'd always preferred to pay for a shot of rum for a drunk than give a cigarette to a beggar, reflected for a moment and told himself he liked the dignified way the old man had made his request. The nails of the hand awaiting the cigarette were pink and clean.

"Here you are, granddad."

"Thanks, son. So we've got wreathes today, have we?"

"Yes, quite a lot," agreed the Count as the old guy lit up. "Do you come here often?"

The old man lifted up his can of coffee.

"I buy five *reales* worth of coffee and it keeps me going to night-time. Who died today? He must be a bigwig. There aren't usually so many flowers," he said, lowering his voice as if to confide a secret. "The fact is flowers are in short supply and that's why wreathes are too and sometimes there's such a dearth I've seen loads of wakes without flowers. Not that it bothers me, not likely. When I die, I'm not worried if I get flowers or cow shit. The guy who died today was a high up, wasn't he?"

"Not really," allowed the Count.

"Well, that's beside the point as well, he's fucked, the poor chap. Thanks for the smoke," said the old man, back to his usual tone, as he continued his descent.

"He's madder than a March hare," commented Manolo.

"Not really," allowed the Count a second time, as he saw a car from headquarters draw up by one side of the park – and he remembered what had set off the headache neither the rich mix of two analgesics nor several layers of Chinese pomade had managed to subdue. Four men got out of the car, two in uniform. Fabricio got out the back door and the Count was pleased to see him in plain clothes, because right then he'd thought there are things men have always had to settle in the same way, and that particular story was due its final chapter now. Let's see how we play it, he thought.

"Wait here," he told Manolo and went down to the street.

"Where you? . . ." the sergeant started to ask, when he understood what the Count intended. He dropped his cigarette and ran in the opposite direction, into the undertakers.

The Count crossed the narrow street that separated the undertakers from the park and went over to the group of men coming from the car. He pointed a finger at Fabricio.

"We didn't finish our conversation earlier on," he said gesturing to him to separate out from the group.

Fabricio moved away from his companions and followed the Count to a corner of the park.

"Well then, what are you after?" the Count asked, who at that split second remembered how years ago he'd had his last fist-fight to defend his food in a school camp, and had been helped by Red Candito. He should be grateful to him to this day that the three thieves hadn't made mincemeat of him. "Tell me, Fabricio, what you got against me?"

"Hey, Conde, who the hell do you think you are? You think you're better than anybody else or what? . . ."

"Hey, I don't think I'm anything at all. What *are* you after?" he repeated and, without thinking what he was

237

doing, threw a punch at Fabricio's face. He wanted to hit him, feel him come apart in his hands, do him damage and not see or hear him again. Fabricio tried to dodge the blow, but Conde's fist caught the side of his neck and made him stagger backwards, and then Conde's left hand smashed into his shoulder. Fabricio responded with a backhander that hit his attacker in the middle of the face. A distant fire, he thought he'd forgotten, exploded in Conde's cheeks: blows to the face enraged him and his arms were now two flailing windmills punching the red mass he could see opposite, until an alien force intervened to lift him up and suspend him in the air: Major Rangel had succeeded in catching him by the armpits and only then did the Count notice the ring of students that had formed around them to egg them on.

"Go on, hit him on the jaw."

"Fuck, great punch."

"I'm betting on Striped Shirt."

"Hit him! Hit him!"

And a hoarse voice, shouting in his ear, in a tone he didn't recognize.

"I'm going to have to kill you, you idiot," and then an immediately changed inflection almost whispering: "It's all right now. It's all right."

"Look, Mario Conde, I'm not going to argue with you about what happened. I don't even want to hear about it. I'd prefer not to see you, you bastard. I know you loved Jorrín, that you're uptight, that you're a neurotic fellow, I even know that Fabricio is an arsehole, but there's no forgiving what you did, and I at least will never forgive you, even though I love you like a son. I – will-not-forgive-you – get it? Give me your lighter. I think I lost mine in the fight you started. It's the only smoke I've got left and the burial's tomorrow morning. Poor Jorrín, Jesus fucking wept! No, don't speak, I said, let me light up. Here's your lighter. Hey, didn't I tell you to keep as quiet as a nun? Didn't I warn you I didn't want any problems? And look what you do: slugging it out with an officer in the middle of the street, in front of an undertakers packed with people from headquarters. Are you mad or an arsehole? Or both? . . . All right, we'll leave this to later, and prime your arse for a good caning. I'm warning you. And don't wipe more Chinese pomade over your forehead because it won't make me take pity on you . . . Fuck, you're over forty and still behaving like a young kid . . . Look, Conde, we'll leave this to later. Now try to do your job properly. You can do that, I know. Take it easy tonight and tomorrow, after the wake, pick this boy up from his house. By that time we should know what the peasant from Escambray knows, the one Orlando San Juan mentioned. The boy has classes in the afternoon, right? Well, bring him along here and Cicerón's gang will check out his house for drugs, because that's probably where the Russian keeps it. But remember he's a boy from Pre-Uni, so easy does it, a firm hand and a tight leash and dig out the name of the midwife who brought him into the world. We need to know whether Lando was in a relationship with the teacher or if it was the boy who brought drugs into the teacher's house, and we need to know how much the drugs circulated in Pre-Uni. The Pre-Uni business terrifies me, it's shit-scary . . . And I think you're right, the marijuana lead will solve the murder, because it would be a big coincidence if the drugs person weren't the murderer, in a case where at the end of the day there's been neither theft nor robbery, and I don't give a fuck for coincidences. Your face hurts. Well, too bad. I wanted Fabricio to knock the living daylights out of you, which is what I'd like to do. Go, move yourself, and get your act together, because now you're going to obey my orders to the letter or I'll stop calling myself Antonio Rangel. Look: I'll swear to it right now, on my mother's life."

Depression still weighed heavily on his shoulders as he slumped on his bed and closed his eyes in the hope that his headache would disappear. Depression was a burden for wrists, knees, neck and ankles, all acting as if exhausted by the huge task. He hadn't the strength to rebel and shout out "Shit, fucking shit", "Go to bloody hell", or to try to forget everything. Depression had only one cure that he knew of: company.

When he left headquarters the Count was already laid low by that nightmarish depression. He knew he'd violated the code, but an even more deeply rooted code had launched him at Fabricio. So he stopped off at a bar, then understood, from his first gulp, that solitary flight down the alcohol trail didn't make any sense either. He felt alien to the joys and sorrows of the other inmates who delved deeper into their necessary confessions with each shot: rum was an emetic for doubts and hopes, not a simple potion to herald in oblivion. That's why he paid, left a half-full glass and went home.

In search of possible relief, the Count dialled for the very first time the number Karina had given him, eight days ago, when they'd met next to a punctured Polish Fiat. His memory successfully reclaimed the number: the ring was faint and distant.

"Yes," said a woman's voice. Karina's mother?

"Can I please speak to Karina."

"She's not been here today. Who's that?"

"A friend," he replied. "When will she be back?"

"Oh, I couldn't say . . ."

A pause, a silence, the Count thinking.

"Could you take down a number?"

"Yes, wait a moment . . ." she must be looking for the wherewithal, "right, go on."

"409213."

"Four-zero-nine-two-one-three," the voice checked.

"Huh-huh. Tell her Mario will be back after eight. And will be expecting a call."

"All right."

"Thanks a lot," and he hung up.

He made an effort and got to his feet. On the way to the lavatory he undressed, dropping clothes everywhere. He stepped on the shower tray and before submitting to the torture of a cold shower glanced through the small window. Outside twilight falling. The wind still stirring up dust, dirt and melancholy. Inside hatred and sadness had ground to a halt. Would it always be thus?

As he walked past Karina's house, the Count noted the orangey Polish Fiat wasn't there. It was a quarter to eight, but he decided he'd have plenty of time to worry later. He looked at the window in the porch, not intending espionage, and only saw the same ferns and *malangas*, turned a golden yellow by the light of a brightly burning lamp.

The door to Skinny's house was open as usual and the Count walked in, asked: "What time they serve dinner in this place?" And he went as far as the kitchen where Skinny and Josefina, like minstrels in vaudeville, were waiting for him hands on head and eyes goggling, as if to say: "It can't be".

"No, it can't be," said Skinny, with the intonation of the character he was performing and finally with a smile. "You telepathic?"

The Count walked over to Josefina, kissed her on the forehead and asked emphasizing his innocence, "What did I tell foretell?"

"Can't you smell it, lad?" the woman asked and then the Count carefully – as if on the edge of a precipice – peered into the top of the pot on the stove.

"No, it's not true, casseroled *tamal*!" he shouted and realized his headache had gone and that depression had a cure.

"Yes, my love, but it's not just any *tamal*: it's made from grated maize, that's much better than if it's been ground, and I sieved it so there were no bits and added marrow to give it body and it's also got pork meat, chicken and beef chops."

"Bloody hell! And look what I've got here," he said, taking a bottle of rum out of its cardboard cone: "three-year-old Caney, golden and smooth."

"Well, in that case I think you can consider yourself invited," Skinny opined, swaying his head from side to side, as if seeking approval from a bevy of guests. "And where did you fish that out from, savage?"

Conde looked at Josefina and put his arm round her shoulders.

"Better not know, because you're no policeman, are

243

you, Josefina?" and she smiled, and gripped Conde's chin and tilted his face.

"What did you cop there, Condesito?"

Conde put the bottle down on the table.

"It's nothing, I fell out with a mop. You know, I stepped . . ." and he tried to mime the origins of the scratch that Fabricio's ring had left on his cheek.

" . . . Hey, savage, you telling the truth?"

"Come on, Skinny, forget it . . . Do you want rum or don't you?" he asked looking at the clock. It was about to strike eight. She must be about to ring.

The background music indicated the heartache brought by the Brazilian soap was over for the night, but the Count appealed to the clock: half past nine. He flopped his head back on the pillow, exhausted, and held out his glass when he heard Skinny pouring himself more.

"That's the end of that," he announced, as if he was the bearer of bad tidings. "You've had a hell of a bad day, haven't you?"

"And then there's what the Boss has got in store. And that youngster tomorrow. And the whore who doesn't ring. What's she got up to, pal?"

"Hey, stuff the whining, she'll turn up . . ."

"It's all too much, Skinny, too much. I realized that when the Boss told me to leave the youth's questioning to tomorrow and I agreed. I should have gone after him today, but I wanted to see her. What a fucking disaster."

The Count sat up and sipped the last drops of rum from the bottom of his glass. As usual, he regretted not buying another bottle: those 750 millilitres didn't satisfy the hardened veins of that pair of high alcoholic averages. Because he'd already downed half a bottle of rum and his thirst remained unslaked, even keener, and he felt he'd been drinking doubt and despair rather than alcohol. How much more would he have to drink before he could finally look over the edge of the canal and slosh over into a lack of consciousness, the object yet again of his consuming thirst?

"I feel like getting plastered, Skinny," he said dropping his glass on the mattress. "Plastered like an animal, crawling on all fours and pissing my pants and not thinking about my life ever again. Never ever . . ."

"Yes, I reckon it's just what you need," the other agreed finishing his rum. "And it was good stuff, you know? One of the few rums that can still hold its head up high in this world. You know it's the real Bacardi?"

"Yeah, I know the story: it's the best in the world, the only genuine Bacardi they make and so on. Right now I couldn't give a fuck: any rum will do. I want 90% proof, dry wine, meths, purslane wine, rat poison, anything that will go straight to my head."

"You're far gone, aren't you? I told you the other day:

245

you're like a bloody lovesick dog. And the woman's not back from work yet. You tell me if she gives you . . ."

"Don't even mention the possibility. I don't want to think about it. Come on, give me money to make it up. I'll kick up a fuss until I find a litre somewhere," he said as he stood up. He looked for the cardboard cone he'd brought and put away the empty bottle.

Josefina was in the living room watching the *Write and Read* programme. The panellists had to identify a twentieth-century, historical, Latin-American figure, and Cuban into the bargain! An artist, they'd just discovered.

"It must be Pello the Afrokán," said the Count going over to Josefina. "Did you get it, Jose?"

Josefina shook her head, keeping her eyes glued to the set.

"Ay, my love, I've been sitting here for two days. Look who the historic figure was," she said, pointing her chin at the screen. "Chorizo the clown. That's an insult to those clever professors who know so much."

Before leaving, the Count kissed her forehead and said he'd soon be back – with more rum.

He stopped on the corner of the street and hesitated. To his left bars summoned, and to his right Karina's place. There was only a lorry parked in front of the whole block and he raised his hopes thinking a Polish Fiat might be lurking behind it. He turned right, passed by the girl's house that was still shut up and saw there was nothing behind the lorry. He walked to the corner, turned half round and walked back past her house. He wanted to go in, ring, ask – I'm a policeman, for fuck's sake, where's she got to? – but a last ounce of pride and commonsense repressed his adolescent impulse when he put his hand on the garden gate. He walked on down the street, after rum and oblivion.

"Well, pal, she didn't ring," he managed to say with enough strength to raise his arm and drink some more. The second bottle of firewater was also practically dead when the National Anthem blared out to mark the end of the evening's programmes.

Josefina stood in the doorway, observed the hecatomb and crossed herself mechanically: the two were shirtless, and gripping their glasses tight. Her son, slumped over the arm of his wheelchair, his flabby flesh streaming with sweaty. And the Count, sitting on the floor, back against the bed, suffering the last rattle from a coughing attack. On the ground, an ashtray steaming like a volcano and the corpses of two bottles and the epilogue to another.

"You're killing yourselves," she said picking up the bottle of firewater. She fled. Those scenes filled her heart with sadness because she knew she spoke the truth: they were committing suicide, cowardly but surely. And only love and loyalty remained from the times when Skinny and the Count spent their evenings and nights in that same room, listening to music at a superhuman volume and arguing about girls and baseball.

"She didn't ring. I'm going for fuck's sake."

"Are you mad? How can you go in that state?"

"Not dragging my bum across the floor. Walking," and he made an unlikely effort to revert to the vertical. He failed twice, but succeeded at the third attempt.

"Are you really leaving?"

"Yes, you beast, I'm throwing myself out. I'll die like a stray dog. Just remember one thing: I fucking love you to death. You're my brother, friend and you're my skinny little pal," he said and, abandoning his glass on the night table, he hugged his pal's sweaty head and gave his hair a slobbering kiss, while Skinny's massive hands gripped the arms that hugged him as the kiss turned into a hoarse, sickly sob.

"Hell, brother, don't cry . . . Nobody deserves your tears. Castrate Fabricio, kill her, forget Jorrín, but don't cry, otherwise I'll cry too."

"Cry then, you bastard. I can't stop myself."

The wind blew from the south, bringing the smell of withered flowers and burnt oil, the effluvia of deaths from yesteryear and yesterday, as cars and buses halted in the cemetery's main avenue. The funeral car had driven a few yards on to allow the mourners to show off their years of experience and form an improvised,

248

disciplined queue, without numbers or fear of being left empty-handed, ready to follow the coffin to its final resting-place. The queue was headed by Jorrín's wife and two children who the Count didn't know, then Major Rangel and other high-ranking officers, all wearing uniforms and stripes. It was far too sad a spectacle for the Count's tender sensitivities: his head, liver, heart and soul hurt; and when they were level with the cemetery's main chapel, he told Manolo, "Go on, I'll catch you up," and he separated out from the procession that advanced like a sleepy snake. The sun was hurting Conde's eyes, breached his sunglasses, and he sought out the shadow of a weeping willow and sat down on one side of the pavement. He was one of the few officers who hadn't come to the ceremony in full uniform and he changed the angle of his pistol as he flopped on the low wall. The silence in the cemetery was intense and the Count was grateful. He had enough noises inside himself and declined to listen to the more or less predictable eulogy that would wind up the mourning for Captain Jorrín. A good father, good policeman, and good colleague? You don't come to a cemetery to learn what you already know. He lit a cigarette and, the other side of the chapel, saw a group of women changing the flowers on a grave and dusting the gravestone. It seemed a social rather than meditative act and the Count remembered he'd been told about the existence of a Miraculous One, in

249

that cemetery, and that people often came to ask for mysterious help from her understanding spirit that was in step with the times. He stood up and went over to the women. Three sat on a bench next to the grave and two were still cleaning briskly, sweeping up leaves and earth left by the wind, re-arranging bunches of flowers in the earthenware jugs. All wore black scarves round their heads, dressed like timeless Spanish village women, swapping more or less accurate rumours about up-and-coming reductions in the weekly egg quota price increases. Without asking their permission the Count sat on the bench next to the women and looked at the grave and the flowers, candles, black rosary beads and blurred picture of a woman behind a glass frame.

"She's the Miraculous One, isn't she?" the policeman asked the nearest woman.

"Yes, sir."

"And you look after the grave?"

"It's our turn once a month. We clean and tidy it and help people who come to ask for something."

"I want to ask for something," the Count replied.

He didn't look like a pilgrim, so the woman, a black woman well into her sixties with arms of soft ham, looked at him for a second before she spoke.

"She's given lots of evidence of her power. And one day the Church will recognize her for what she is: a miracle-working saint, a creature beloved of the Lord. If you can bring her flowers, candles, things like that, it helps when you ask, because it lights up her path, but all you really need is faith, lots of faith, and then you ask her for help and say a prayer. An Our Father, a Hail Mary, whatever you prefer. And ask from the bottom of your heart, with lots of faith. You understand?"

The Count nodded and remembered Jorrín. They must be saying goodbye to him now; no doubt the Boss, a companion of thirty years standing, would speak of his record of unstinting service to society, family and life. Then he looked at the grave opposite and tried to recall a prayer. If he was going to ask for something, he'd do it properly, trying to recover the scattered bits of the faith he'd reneged on, but he didn't make it past the first lines of the Lord's Prayer that he confused with fragments of Mario Benedetti's *Lord's Prayer for Latin America* – that had become so popular during his time at university, when an urgent Latin Americanization of Cuban culture was decreed and strident rock groups transformed into pathetic, chameleon-like adepts of Andean and Altiplano folklore, panpipes, tambourines and ponchos included, and some even sang in Quechua and Aymara rather than Spanish. But now faith was what was crucial. Which faith? I'm atheist, but I have faith. In what? In almost nothing. Too much of a pessimist to have space for faith. But you'll help me, Miraculous One, won't you? Huh-huh. I'll only ask for one thing, though it's a very big

251

one, and as you work miracles, you'll help me, because I need a miracle as big as this cemetery to get what I want, you understand? . . . I hope so and that you're hearing me: I want to be happy. Is that so much to ask for? I hope not, but don't forget, Miraculous One, all right?

"Thanks a lot," he said to the black woman when he stood up. She'd been looking at him all that time and smiled.

"Come back whenever you want, sir."

"I think I might," he said waving at the women, who'd switched from the topic of eggs to the chickens that had yet to reach the butchers. The usual story: the chicken or the egg? He walked back to the central avenue and, on his right, saw the mourners coming back from the burial. He adjusted his glasses and went to look for the car, hoping he'd be able to sit down. He felt weak and ridiculous and he knew he was going soft. It's as if I were in meltdown. Bloody shit. He tried his door but it was locked like Manolo's. He saw the radio aerial on the back seat. He distrusts even the dead, he thought. And then thought: will she grant me my miracle?

"How did it go?"

Greco, in uniform, was waiting for them under the almond tree planted by the entrance to the parking lot at headquarters. He barely saluted when Conde came over and replied.

"Plain sailing. We got to his house at eight, as Manolo told us, called in his mother, explained it was a routine investigation connected to Orlando San Juan, and then called him in – he was still asleep. The search carried out by Cicerón's people brought nothing to light, Conde."

"What did you make of him?"

"He's a bit loud-mouthed and protested to start with, but I think it's pure show."

"Did you tell him anything else?"

"No, not a thing. Crespo's with him upstairs in your cubbyhole. It's all set up as per instructions."

"Up we go, Manolo," he then said and they went into a building that was quiet at a time when it was usually bustling. They found the lift waiting for them, doors open, in the lobby. Miracles already? wondered the Count and pressed the button to his floor. When they were in the corridor, Manuel Palacios took a deep breath and filled his lungs, like a deep-sea diver about to take the plunge.

"Shall we begin?"

"Be tough," said the Count following him.

Manolo opened the door to the cubicle where bald Crespo and Lázaro San Juan were sitting. Crespo stood up and saluted Manolo with almost a martial air.

"Bring him here, Crespo," asked the sergeant.

Still in the corridor, the Count saw the boy come out. He was handcuffed and he'd lifted his hands to his forehead.

"Take off the handcuffs," he ordered Crespo and looked at Lázaro San Juan's face; although it bore no similarity to Lando the Russian's, family traits were in evidence – an apparently absent gaze and almost straight, lipless mouth. He looked older than a youth who'd just celebrated his eighteenth birthday. His body was endowed with a firm, adult bone structure, and layered in rippling muscle. A few spots on his face betrayed his youth, but not even the red acne pimples obscured his masculine grace. His hair was parted down the middle and he didn't seem scared. Lissette was a woman who ate well and badly with equal relish, because it was a way to eat twice. That boy must have been her favourite dish, thought Conde. Tough on the digestion.

They processed awkwardly along the corridor and entered the lift. They went up to the next floor and walked out into a similar corridor, one lined with glass and aluminium doors. They went through two doorways and opened a wooden door that led into the tiniest of cubicles that was in semi-darkness. There was a curtain down one side. Manolo pointed Lázaro to the only chair and the youngster sat down. Crespo switched the light on.

"Lázaro San Juan Valdés?" asked Manolo and the youngster nodded. "An eleventh grade student at La Víbora Pre-Uni, correct?"

"Yes," he answered.

"All right, do you know why you're here?"

The youngster looked around him, as if trying to get an idea of where he was.

"I was told it was an investigation into Pre-Uni."

"Do you know or can you imagine what kind of investigation?"

"I think it's to do with Lissette the teacher. I was in the lavatories the other day when your colleague came in and asked about her." He replied looking at Conde.

"That's right," Manolo continued, "it's about her. Lissette the teacher was murdered on Tuesday the eighteenth, at around midnight. She was strangled with a towel. Someone had sexual contact with her just before. Someone gave her a good beating just before. But before that, lots of alcohol was drunk in her place and marijuana smoked. What can you tell us about any of that?"

The youngster looked back at Conde, who'd lit a cigarette.

"Nothing, comrade, how could I?"

"Are you sure? Call Greco," Manolo addressed Crespo. The policeman picked a phone up and whispered something. He hung up. In the meantime, Manolo leafed through a small notebook he was holding and opted to read, an apparently enthralling read, while the Count smoked and looked all casual, as if present at a very familiar performance. Seated in the centre of the tiny room, Lázaro San Juan shifted his gaze from one to the other, as if waiting for them to award him a deferred mark in a final examination. Doubt grew in his gaze, for all to see, like a well-nourished weed.

Two knocks on the wooden door, and in walked Greco's sharp-pointed bones. I'm surrounded by skin and bones. I'm even turning skin and bones, recalled the Count. Greco was carrying a piece of paper. He handed it to the Count and left. The lieutenant glanced at it and nodded, when he looked up at Manolo. Lázaro San Juan's gaze flew from one to the other. Still waiting for his mark.

"All right, Lázaro, we'll get down to the serious stuff. On the eighteenth you were in the house of your teacher Lissette. Your fingerprints are there. And it's very likely you were the one who went to bed with her that night: your blood is group O, the same as the man whose semen she had in her vagina when she died." Manolo walked towards the curtain which was to the left of Lázaro, drew it back to reveal the translucent glass that, as in a game of mirrors, gave a to-scale reproduction of the room where they were, but with less backdrop, action and characters. "Your cousin, Orlando San Juan, sits in there, accused of possessing and peddling drugs, attempted illegal departure from the country and the theft of a motor launch belonging to the State. He has confessed to all his crimes and told us moreover that on the eighteenth, at around 7.30 p.m., you went to his house and stayed there for a while. Moreover it transpires that the marijuana your cousin possesses is the same kind as the stuff that turned up in the toilet in Lissette's place. As you can see, Lázaro, you're more trapped up in this tale of drugs and murder than mincemeat in a pie. Even if you don't confess, any court will have a ball with all these facts I've given you. What's more, the colleague who brought me these papers has just gone to get Luis Gustavo Rodríguez and Yuri Samper, your little Pre-Uni friends, and when we talk to them, you bet they will confirm lots of things. OK, as you can see, very serious stuff. You got anything to say?"

The Count watched the mutation take place. It was like a wave that advanced from the guts and surfaced through the skin. Lázaro's muscles lost their ripple and his chest deflated. His hair was no longer neatly parted down the middle, but awry like a badly fitting wig. The spots on his face turned dark and he no longer seemed beautiful, strong or young and instinct told the Count that they'd reached the epilogue to that tale. Why would he have killed her? Why would an eighteen-year-old youth do something so bestial and definitive as that? Why could the quest for happiness end in that degeneration that had only just begun and would never finish, not even after the ten, fifteen years Lázaro San Juan was going to spend surrounded by the degrading

257

rigours of prison life, by murderers like himself, thieves, rapists and conmen, who would fight over the dark heart of his beauty and youth like a trophy they would sooner or later devour with great pleasure. No miracle would save this Lazarus.

"All right, all that's true, except for the idea I killed her and went to bed with her, I swear on my mother. I didn't kill her and wasn't with her either that day, and Luis and Yuri will tell you that's so, you'll see. Yes, she thought up the party, told me about it during break at Pre-Uni, hey Lacho – that's what she called me – you know what? Why don't you drop by tonight for a while, I'll have rum? She and I, you know, were an item for a few months, from December, she partied with me and I'm only human and we started to go to bed, but nobody knew in Pre-Uni, and I told only Luis and Yuri and they swore not to tell, and that was it, nobody knew. Then I told them, come one, let's go and have a drink or two, and had the bright idea of going to Lando's and stealing a few of the joints he liked smoking, I knew he put them inside a packet of Marlboro, one of the cardboard kind, in a pocket in his jacket in his bedroom, because I saw him take one from there once and I went and stole a few but only two or three times. And that was all, I met up with my pals on the street corner near her house and we went up at about eight-thirty, started to drink, listen to music and dance and I lit a joint and we smoked but she didn't because she said she wanted more rum. Yuri went as far as El Niágara and bought two more bottles with the money she'd given him, and that was all, she was half drunk when we left at about eleven, we were incredibly hungry because she never had any food in the house, and we went to the stop and caught our buses, they the number 15 and me the 174, that drops me nearer my house, and that was all, that was that. We found out the next day and were incredibly scared and decided it would be better not to say anything to anybody, because somebody would jump to conclusions, like you have. That was all, I swear to you. I didn't kill her or go to bed with her that night. I swear I didn't. You ask Yuri and Luis who were with me, you ask them, go on . . ."

Far too many mysteries by half, the Count told himself. He wanted to think about the mystery concocted around Lissette's death, but the unexpected riddle of Karina's disappearance kept getting in the way, where could she have got to last night, he rang her again after speaking to Lázaro and the same female voice as on the previous night spoke to him: "No, she didn't come here yesterday, but she phoned and I gave her your message. She didn't ring you?" That statement was like a gust coming from the poop deck, swelling the sails of his doubts and fears and setting them off at top speed across a choppy, uncertain Sargasso Sea. He knew the company Karina worked for was based in El Vedado, but his enthusiasm prevented him doing his policeman thing and he'd never asked her for her exact address, after all, she lived around the corner from Skinny, and he didn't dare ask the woman at the other end of the line. Karina's mother? Something irrevocable had happened, as on the night of the eighteenth, he thought. Leaning against the window in his office, he looked at the defiant crests of the weeping figs and their evergreen leaves that resisted everything. He wished time would fly, so he could go home and wait next to his phone. She'd ring him with a good excuse, he tried to tell himself. I was on duty and forgot to tell you. We had a work crisis and I stayed back, and you know how terrible the phones are, I couldn't get through, my love. But he knew he was lying to himself. A miracle? Only a miracle of springtime, old Machado would say, also touched by a love that finally eluded him.

He heard someone open his office door. Manolo, carrying a sheaf of papers, flopped down in the big chair, imitating the exhaustion of a victorious runner. He was laughing.

"It's a real pity about the lad, but he's shot it, Conde."

"He's shot it?" asked the lieutenant, allowing the flow of his thoughts to get back on track. "What has the laboratory got to tell us?"

"The semen belongs to Lázaro. No doubt about that."

"And Yuri and Luis?"

"What you'd thought, they caught the bus first and left Lázaro at the stop. They say they always went together to the stop in La Víbora and then got off to go to Acosta Avenue, but that night he told them to go, that he was going to catch the 174 so as not to have to walk so far."

"And the white shirt?"

"Yes, it was his and he'd taken it that night. She'd sometimes wash clothes for him. Poor Lázaro, and he had it all on a plate, didn't he?"

"Yes, poor Lázaro, he doesn't know what will hit him. And what did they tell you about the party?"

"It was different to the one Lázaro invented. They say that when she got drunk she got very stroppy because Lázaro told her to give him the physics and maths exams and she started to talk straight, she wouldn't give him any more exams, because he played the big man with everyone else saying what was going to come up and he would get her into trouble, that was all he wanted her for, apart from *it*, they say she said, and then told them to clear off. Luis says it's true Lázaro used to sell the answers to the exam questions, but she didn't know. Sly sod, wasn't he? Well, Lázaro tried to calm her down but she insisted on the three of them going, and even almost pushed Lázaro out when Yuri and Luis were already on the stairs. They both told the same story, step by step. Then, when they found out about the teacher's death they went to talk to Lázaro and decided it would be best

261

not to say they'd been there that night. They thought it best in order not to create problems for themselves, but Yuri says it was Lázaro's idea they should keep quiet."

The Count lit a cigarette and glanced briefly at the data Manolo had brought from the central laboratories. He left them on the table and went back to his window, stared at a single scrap of skyline and said: "Then Lázaro went back from the bus stop. He didn't have a key, so she opened the door. He persuaded her she'd made a mistake and they had sex on the living room sofa. A great reconciliation, I can almost hear the background music. But why did he kill her?" he wondered, and lost sight of the scrap of skyline he'd selected when he saw Lázaro on Lissette, saw his face at last, as he tightened the towel round her throat, tighter and tighter, until his oarsman's arms slackened after all that effort and the enigmatically beautiful face of the girl locked for ever in that absurd rictus, between pain and uncertainty. Why did he kill her?

The blue smoke smells like spring: fresh and sharp. Steamy and evanescent, the smokes floats from mouth to lungs, from lungs to brain and dawns behind the eyes; which perceive the glint of a new day in everything, a heightened perception and sensitivity revealing shafts of mother-of-pearl lucidity never grasped before. The world, the whole world, becomes broader and nearer, and shiny, while the smoke disperses, transforms into breath lost to each blood cell and neuron that is awake and on full alert. Life is beautiful, isn't it, people are beautiful, your hands are big, your arms powerful, your knob huge. Thanks, smoke.

Marijuana was among the things Christopher Columbus discovered without imagining he had. Those Indians "with charred sticks in their mouths" looked too happy to be mere smokers of tobacco on the verge of emphysema. Dried grass, dark leaves, blue smoke that made it possible to mistake sad, disconsolate Columbus for a pinkish god out of a mystery lost in the Indians' mythical memory. A good joint. A leaf too lethal by far when they discovered that Columbus wasn't God, and they weren't his chosen spirits.

But smoking it is a pleasure, is to float over the dust of hours and days, knowing we are all powerful: able to create and believe, to be and not to be where nobody can be and not be, while the imagination soars as blue as the smoke and breathing is easy, seeing is easy, listening supreme joy.

Poor Lázaro, he'll go to the bonfire like an Indian, without blue smoke or dawn lights, already sentenced to the first space in the seventh circle of hell, to burn eternally with those who've wrought violence on their neighbour.

He walked into the boss's secretary's office and was surprised by Maruchi's smile. She waved at him, wait,

wait, stop, and tiptoed from behind her desk over to the Count.

"What's got into you, my girl?"

"Keep your voice down, young man," she insisted, her hands urging him to lower the volume, as she whispered. "Hey, he's in there with Cicerón and Fatman Contreras and he asked me to take them coffee. Do you know what they were talking about when I went in?"

"About a corpse."

"About you, young man."

"About a corpse," confirmed the lieutenant.

"Don't be silly. He was telling Fatman and Cicerón you'd put them both on the trail of two big cases. That you'd uncovered. What do you reckon?"

"The Count tried to smile but failed.

"Very nice."

"Ugh, don't be so boring . . ." she said assuming her normal tone of voice.

"Tell him I'm here, go on."

The head of office returned to her desk and pressed her red intercom button. A tinny voice asked "Yes?" and she announced his presence: "Major, Lieutenant Conde is here."

"Tell him to come in," the metallic voice replied.

"Maruchi, thanks for the headlines," said the Count and he stroked the secretary's hair. She smiled, a flattered smile that surprised the Count. Could this darling really fancy him? He went over to the glass door and rapped it with his knuckles.

"Go on, come in," shouted the Major, and the Count opened the door.

Wearing his uniform and official decorations, the Boss was standing behind his desk as if commiserating over another deceased – "me," thought the lieutenant, with the two mourners opposite: Captains Contreras and Cicerón.

"You're in good company," he quipped to relieve the tension, and saw Fatman Contreras smile as he stood up, his veins swelling as he suddenly hauled up his three hundred pounds of flesh and bone.

"How are you, Conde?" And he held out his hand. Shit you, thought the lieutenant, dropping his poor hand on Contreras's, whose smile broadened when he unleashed all his pressure on the Count's defenceless fingers.

"Fine, Captain."

"All right, sit yourselves down," the Boss ordered. "Well now, Conde, where are you at with your case?"

The Count sat in the sofa that was to the Major's right. He put the envelope he'd brought down by his side and tapped it before replying.

"It's all here. I brought the tapes in case you want to hear them. And tomorrow the public prosecutor will receive our report."

"That's all fine and dandy, but what did you turn up?"

"Lázaro San Juan, just as we thought. The party took place, with two other friends, they drank rum, smoked marijuana and she rowed with Lázaro when he asked her for the physics and maths exams. The problem was that Lázaro sold the exam answers for five pesos a time. It was a good deal, because there were the answers to as many as ten questions and he had a select, faithful clientele."

"Don't be sarcastic," the Major interjected.

"I'm not being sarcastic."

"Yes, you are."

"I swear I'm not, Boss."

"I told you never to swear anything in front of me."

"Well, I won't."

"Well, are you going to continue with your report or not?"

"I'll continue," sighed the Count, delaying before lighting up another cigarette. "She kicked them out of the house, that was her drunken state talking, it seems, but Lázaro went back after his friends caught their bus. She opened up for him, they made up, had sex and he lit another joint he'd brought along. They smoked it between them, always from his hand, that's why there were no traces on her fingers. And then he asked her for the exams again. The bastard had got the habit. She dug her heels in and tried to kick him out again and he says she struck him in the face and he lost his temper and

266

went for her, started hitting her and before he realized it had strangled her. He says he doesn't know how he could. Sometimes these things happen, being high on loads of dope doesn't help . . . now he's crying. It was an effort, but he's crying. I'm sorry for the kid, he made his confession without looking at us. He asked me to let him stand by the window and talked the whole time staring into the street. It's not going to be easy for him. It's all here," he repeated tapping the envelope again, which sounded like a warning drumbeat in the silence.

"A pretty tale, is it not?" asked the Boss getting to his feet. "A boy at Pre-Uni and his teacher as protagonists and a headmaster, a dealer in stolen motorbikes and dope peddler in supporting roles; a bit of everything: sex, violence, drugs, crime, alcohol, fraud, currency swindles, black-marketing, sexual favours and just deserts," he said and suddenly switched his tone. "It makes you want to vomit. Tomorrow I'll have your report sent everywhere, Conde, everywhere . . ."

And he went back to his seat and the battered cigar he'd been fighting all afternoon. It was a sad, dark cheroot, all dark ash and acrid aroma. He took two drags, as if taking a necessary but foul medicine, and said:

"Contreras and Cicerón have been telling me about the case's other ramifications. That Pupy sang so much they almost had to kick him to shut him up. We got further up the pole thanks to him, to three functionaries working in foreign embassies, two fellows from Cubalse, the wholesale people, three from INTERTUR, two taxi drivers and a load of pimps."

"Eight for starters," smiled Contreras.

"And the marijuana racket is a fuse that keeps burning and we'll watch where it takes us. The peasant from Escambray seems straight out of some film scenario: they supplied him with drugs to sell as his own to various dealers like Lando. We've caught three more. And we'll get the man in Trinidad who supplied the peasant and we'll go on until the bomb explodes, because we've got to find out where that marijuana came from and how it got into Cuba, because this time I don't swallow the story about how they found it washed up on the seashore. Until the bomb explodes . . ."

"And the shit hits the fan," whispered the Count very quietly.

"What was that?" asked the Major.

"Nothing, Boss."

"But what did you say that I didn't catch?"

"That the shit will hit the fan. And not only in La Víbora Pre-Uni."

"Shit will hit the fan, right," agreed the Major as he tried in vain to get a drag out of his blackened cigar. "And it's coming my way already," he said, looking appalled and showing the ersatz cigar to them all. He stood up, walked over to the window and threw the cigar into the street, as if he hated it. Which, of course, he did. When the Major turned his back to the group, Cicerón looked at the Count and smiled: raised his right arm and gave a V for Victory sign.

The Major went back to his desk and leaned his knuckles on the wood. The Count prepared himself for his harangue.

"Although it goes against the grain, Conde, I have to congratulate you. You were the person who unravelled the piece-of-shit stories we got from Pupy and Lando and you solved the Pre-Uni business. The currency swindle and purchases from diplomatic shops will bring in other people and the Central American marijuana will take us into the stratosphere, I'm quite sure, because this is no low-level operation. So I congratulate you on all these fronts, but tomorrow after you've delivered your report, I want you to go home, make yourself comfortable, in pyjamas and all, and don't you show your face back here until the disciplinary committee calls you in."

"But Rangel . . ." Contreras tried to interject only to be interrupted in turn by the Boss.

"Contreras, you can tell the Committee what you think. I couldn't care less. The Count did something to his credit and I congratulated him and I'll put it on his file. Besides that's why he's paid. But he played it wrong and fouled up. That's clear enough. The three of you can go. Back here at nine, Conde," he said and slowly flopped into his chair. He pressed his white intercom button and asked: "Maruchi, bring me a glass of water and an aspirin."

The Count, Contreras and Cicerón went out into the hall and the lieutenant whispered to his secretary: "Give him an analgesic. He didn't ask for one because I was there," and walked out.

"Manolo, I'd like to ask you a favour."

"I love you asking favours of me, Conde."

"That's why I do it: draw up the report to give to the Boss in the morning. I want out of here," he said, and opened his hands out to signal the space that was attacking him. The cubicle seemed more than ever like a hot, narrow incubator where he'd burst out of his shell. The feeling that he was at the end of a line and the prospect of having to confront the investigation pointed up by Major Rangel left him in a limbo he'd no purchase on, in which every move was out of his control. He collected together the last papers that were still on his desk and put them in a file.

"Hey, Conde, it can't be so bad, can it?"

"No, it can't be, can it?" he replied, by way of saying something, as he handed the file to his subordinate.

"Don't let them get you down, pal. You know you won't have problems. Cicerón told me as much. I know what you're thinking, Conde: everybody at headquarters is talking about the dirt we've raked up in this case and people are taking bets on which big fish will be wriggling in the net... And Fabricio is known to be an incompetent arsehole, even the cat says so. Besides the major is your best friend and you know it," Manolo argued, trying to soothe an evidently troubled Conde. Although they were two very dissimilar characters, the months they'd been working together had created a mutual dependence they both enjoyed as an extension of their own abilities and desires. Sergeant Manuel Palacios found it hard to believe that tomorrow he'd no longer be working for Lieutenant Mario Conde and would answer to orders from another officer. He wanted the Count to fight back. "Don't worry about the report, I'll write it, but take that look off your face."

The Count smiled: lifted his hands to his chin and began to remove a mask that refused to budge.

"Drop it, Manolo. It's not just this. It's everything. I'm fed up, at the age of thirty-five, and don't know what I'm going to do or what the fuck I want to do. I try to do things right and always end up putting my foot in it: it's my fate, as a *babalao* once told me. I've got the curse of the slug: it all looks beautiful ahead but I leave a trail of slime behind. It's that simple. Look, this is for you," he said and handed him a folded sheet of paper he'd tucked into his shirt pocket.

"What's that?"

271

"An epic-heroic poem I wrote to marijuana. Put it with the report."

"Now you have landed yourself in it, pal."

The Count felt the need to go over to the window and look out – for the last time? – at a landscape that he'd dubbed his favourite, but he thought it wasn't a good moment to say farewell to that piece of the city and that life. He shook the sergeant's hand and shook it vigorously.

"See you, Manolo."

"Do you want me to drive you home?"

"No, don't worry, overloaded buses have grown on me recently."

He didn't feel in the mood to pursue climatic enquiries when he came out into the main lobby at headquarters, but was stirred up by the sunlight insinuating itself through the high windows at the front, and the Count, wanting to assert boundaries and states of mind, looked for his sunglasses. The Lenten wind blew no longer; perhaps it had exhausted its reserves for this year, and a glorious March afternoon greeted him with a clear sky and the perfect brilliance of a postcard spring for tourists fleeing the cold. It was really an ideal afternoon to be by the seaside, close to that house of wood and tiles the Count had occasionally dreamed of owning. He would have spent the morning writing – naturally, a simple, moving tale of love and friendship – and now, with his lines baited up and in the sea, he'd wait for fate to put a fine fish on his hook for tonight's dinner. A woman bronzed by a torrid sun was reading the pages he'd written that day on a nearby rock that jutted out to sea like an outstretched hand. He'd make love with her in the shower when night fell, with the smell of the fish in the oven wafting through the space in that recurrent dream. Perhaps at night, while he read a novel by Hemingway or one of Salinger's immaculate stories, she'd play her saxophone, and bring a sad sound to that blissful scene.

The Polish Fiat was crouching next to the kerb, and the Count noticed its four tyres at rest, full of air. The house door was still shut and the Count walked towards it across the small garden of *marpacíficos* and crotons that had been stripped of their leaves by so many windy days. The iron knocker, wrought like the tongue of an astigmatic lion, raised a deep roar that ran terrified into the house. He took his sunglasses off, settled his revolver against the waistband of his jeans, hoping against hope she had some good excuses. Any good excuse, because he was ready to accept any and ask no questions. At this stage in life he'd learned – practising it in the most objective reality – that to stand excessively on your dignity only brings more hurt: he preferred to demur, forgive, and even promise to forget to obtain the minimal space he required. Why hadn't he let Fabricio's petulance pass him by? He sometimes thought this mean-spirited, but he knew he'd finally acquiesce.

Karina opened the door and didn't look surprised. She even tried to smile and opened a breech he didn't dare cross. She was in the shorts she had worn on the day they had first met and a man's sleeveless shirt that the Count found very titillating. Its armholes slackened to reveal the precise spot where her bosom swelled into a mountain of breast. She'd just washed her hair that fell soft, dark and damp over her shoulders. He was too fond of this woman.

"Come in, I was expecting you," she said, moving to one side. She closed the door and pointed him to one of the wicker chairs set out where the passage leading to the back of the house opened out.

"Are you by yourself?"

"Yes, I just arrived. How's your case going?"

"I think that's fine: I discovered an eighteen-year-old youth who smoked marijuana and killed a twenty-four-year-old girl who also took drugs and had several boyfriends."

"How awful!"

"Not that bad, I've had much worse. What happened to you yesterday?" he finally asked, looking her in the eye. She was on duty. Lots of work. Had to go into hospital. Was taken inside; blame a policeman. Any excuse, for fuck's sake.

"Nothing much," she replied. "I had a phone call."

The Count tried to understand: only one. But understood nothing.

"I don't get you. We'd agreed . . ."

"My husband rang," she replied and the Count thought he'd not understood again. The word "husband" sounded simply ridiculous and out of place in that conversation. A husband? Karina's husband?

"What are you trying to tell me?"

"That my husband gets back tonight. He's a doctor. He's been in Nicaragua. His contract has been ended and he's coming back early. That's what I'm trying to tell you, Mario. He rang me yesterday morning."

The Count searched his shirt-pocket for a cigarette but gave up. He didn't really want to smoke.

"How's that possible, Karina?"

"Mario, don't make things any harder for me. I don't know why I started on this madness with you. I felt alone, I liked you, I needed sex, do hear what I'm saying, but I chose the worst man in the world."

"Am I the worst?"

"You fall in love, Mario," she said, tidying her hair behind her ears. In her shorts and T-shirt, she was like an effeminate boy. He'd always fall in love with her again.

"So what?"

"So I'm going back to my house and my husband, Mario, I can't and don't want to do anything else.

I'm happy I got to know you but I'm sorry, it's not possible."

The Count refused to hear what she was saying. A whore? He thought there must be a mistake, and couldn't find the logic behind any possible mistake. Karina wasn't for him, he concluded. Dulcinea didn't materialize because she didn't exist. Mythology pure and simple.

"I understand," he said finally, and now really did feel he needed a smoke. He dropped the match in a vase full of red-hearted *malangas*.

"I know how you feel, Mario, but it all happened like that, on the spur of the moment. I should never have met you."

"I think we should have met, but at another time, in another place, in another life: because I'd have fallen in love with you just the same. Ring me some time," he said getting up. He lacked arguments and energy to fight the inevitable and knew in advance that he was defeated. He felt he had no option but to accept failure.

"Don't think ill of me, Mario," she replied, also standing up.

"Does it matter to you what I think?"

"Yes, it does. I think you're right, we should meet up in another life."

"Pity about the mistake. But don't worry, I'm always getting it wrong," he said opening the door. The sun was disappearing behind the old Marian Brothers school in

La Víbora and the Count felt like crying. Recently he'd wanted to cry a lot. He looked at Karina and wondered: why? He held her shoulders, stroked her thick, damp hair and kissed her gently on the lips. "Tell me when you need a tyre changing. It's my speciality."

And he walked down the porch towards the garden. He was sure she'd call out, tell him to hell with everything, she'd stay with him, she adored sad policemen, she'd always play her sax for him, he only had to say "play it again", they'd be birds of the night, hungry for love and lust, he heard her run towards him, arms outstretched and sweet music in the background, but each step he took in the direction of the street stuck the knife in a little deeper, quickly bled dry his last hope. When he reached the pavement he was a man alone. What a load of shit, he thought. There wasn't even any music.

Skinny Carlos shook his head. He refused to give up.

"Piss off, you savage. I've not been to the stadium for years and you've got to come. Don't you remember when we used to go? That's right, you went the day Rabbit made it to sixteen and he celebrated with us in the stadium by smoking sixteen cigarettes. The gungy croquettes and brake-fluid mineral water he vomited in the bus looked like volcanic lava, I swear on my mother. It was steaming, kid . . ." and he smiled.

The Count smiled as well. He looked at the posters that had faded over the time, posters that had seen him visit almost every day over so many years. They were witness to Skinny's anti-Beatles crisis, when he converted to the religion of Mick Jagger and The Rolling Stones, from which he then recovered to return to the safe nest of *Rubber Soul* and *Abbey Road* and engage again with the Count in the endless argument pitting McCartney's genius against Lennon's. Skinny was in the McCartney team and the Count was a cheerleader among the dead Lennon's supporters: *Strawberry Fields* was too powerful a lyric not to qualify him as the supreme poet of the Beatles.

"But I don't feel like it, you animal. I just want to flop on my bed, pull the sheet over my head and wake up in ten year's time."

"Rip Van Winkle in this heat? And what'll you do in ten years? You'd be thinner than a bloody rake, still in the same state and would miss out on ten championships, hundreds of bottles of rum and even the odd cello-playing woman. Do you really prefer the sax to the cello? The shittiest bit would be me being so bored out of mind until you woke up."

"Are you trying to console me?"

"No, I'm getting ready to piss on your photo if you carry on being so silly. Let's go and eat. Andrés and Rabbit will be here any minute. I'd like the four of us to go alone to the stadium. It's a man's game, isn't it?"

278

And the Count felt again how he'd lost the will to fight, and let himself be dragged off to his friend's den that was perhaps the only safe place left to him in a war apparently intent on demolishing all his defences and parapets.

"I wasn't inspired today," warned Josefina when they all were seated round the table. "They only had one chicken and I didn't have any brainwaves. But then I remembered that my cousin Estefanía, who'd studied in France, gave me a recipe one day for fried chicken *à la Villeroi*. And I thought, let's see what that's like."

"*A la* what? How do you cook that, Jose?"

"It's real easy, that's why I went for it. I quartered the chicken, and added a bitter orange and two cloves of garlic, and let it marinate. It has to be a big chicken, or it won't work. Then I basted it with half a pound of butter and two sliced onions. They say one onion, but I put in two, and kept remembering the story of the pigs that go to a restaurant. You know the one, don't you? Well, when it's golden brown, you pour on a cup of dry white wine and add salt and pepper. Then it starts to go soft. When it's cold, you de-bone the bird. And that's when the fun really begins: you know how the French do everything with a sauce? This one has butter, milk, salt, pepper and flour. Then you place it on the burner until it becomes a thick, double cream, without lumps. Then more dry wine and lemon juice. You pour half

279

the creamy sauce in a deep serving dish, the other half over the chicken and let it go cold and set, you with me? Then you bread the bits of chicken and it's done: I've just fried them in hot fat. It would be a meal for six French men but you're such a greedy guts . . . Will there be any left for me?"

The smell of the chicken *à la Villeroi* promised pleasures they'd long forgotten. When the Count tasted the first mouthful, he was on the point of being reconciled to life: the sensation that his palate was being born anew with strong, original flavours triggering the illusion that something was being re-shaped within.

"What time are these people picking us up?" he asked Skinny as he tackled the second chicken portion, accompanied by white rice, mashed green plantain and the spring rainbow salad of lettuce, tomato, and carrot seasoned with homemade mayonnaise.

"I don't know, just after seven. Any time now."

"A pity we don't have any white wine," lamented Josefina and she put her knife and fork down for a second. "Hey, Condesito, you know you're my son too, so I can tell you this now: I knew all about Karina, that she was married and so on. I found out straight away here in the barrio. But I didn't think it was any of my business. Perhaps I was wrong and should have said something."

The Count finished swallowing and poured some water into his glass.

"I'm glad you said nothing, Jose. Shall I tell you the truth? Even though it's ended like it has, it was worth it for the three days I spent with her."

"Just as well," said Jose picking up her knife and fork again. "The chicken's not so bad, is it?"

The rediscovered scenario of the stadium brought with it a flood of memories. The green grass shining under bluish light and the reddish turf, freshly raked for the start of the game, created a contrast of colours that is the exclusive heritage of baseball grounds. Andrés walked on in front looking for the box they'd fixed for tonight. Behind, Rabbit opened up space for the wheelchair the Count was pushing with all the skill he'd acquired over ten years. "Pardon me, gentlemen," said Rabbit, who was at the same time trying to watch the Havana pitcher warming up, next to the dugout on the left. The teams were already up on the electronic scoreboard and the murmur descending from the terraces like a waterfall augured a momentous spectacle: Orientales and Havanans were going to engage, once again, as if it were only a game, in a historic contest that perhaps began the day when the colony's capital was transferred from Santiago to Havana almost four hundred years ago.

The box they'd procured through a patient of Andrés' who worked in the INDER was in a most sought-after location: right on the edge of the field, between home-plate and third base. Sitting next to Skinny, the Count gazed at the green and brown terrain, the packed terraces, the colours of the uniforms, blue and white on the one hand, red and black on the other, and remembered that once, like Andrés, he'd decided he'd commit his life to those symbolic realms, where the movement of a tiny ball was like the flux of life, unpredictable but necessary for the game to go on. He'd always liked the loneliness of the centre of the park, the wide open spaces, the responsibility of receiving the solid mass of ball against the skin of the glove, the intellectual shock provoked by an instinctive ability that made him run after the white ball the precise moment it flew from the bat and began its capricious journey.

Those were the smells, colours, sensations, skills that came from a possible attachment to a place and time he could revisit simply by seeing and breathing with relish a unique location, deeply buried in his life experience, as close to his heart as the one he associated with fighting cocks. Earth, sweat, saliva, leather, wood, the sweet green smell of trampled grass and, more than once the taste of blood, were sensations his memory and senses had perfectly assumed and assimilated. The Count breathed peacefully: he owned something, with love and squalor.

"To think I could be down there, right?" said Andrés whom the other three had often gone to cheer on in the stadiums of Havana. At one time he'd been the best baseball player at Pre-Uni and the idea of playing on that five-star ground became a dream they all shared, to the day when Andrés realized his potential didn't in fact extend to achieving such glory.

"I've not been back here for ages," commented Skinny, who was no longer skinny, stroking the arms of his wheelchair.

"Andrés," Rabbit interjected, "what would you want to be if you had your time again?"

Andrés smiled. When he laughed, precocious wrinkles launched a tumultuous demonstration all over his face.

"A baseball player, I reckon."

"And what about you, Carlos?"

Skinny looked at Rabbit and then the Count.

"I don't know. You'd be a historian, but I'm not sure . . . Possibly a musician, but in a nightclub, where they play mambos and such."

"And, Conde, would you be a policeman?"

The Count looked at his three friends. They were happy tonight, like the thirty thousand people on the terraces who'd started to whistle at the referees walking out on the pitch.

"I wouldn't be a baseball player, musician, historian, writer or policeman: I'd be a fucking umpire," he declared, immediately getting up, turning to the pitch and shouting: "Umpire, bastard, piss-taker . . ."

* * *

The moon's reflection came through the panes of glass and traced elusive shapes on the top of the bed that transformed grotesquely as the spectator's perspective shifted. They were forms moulded by solitude. The pillow now seemed an almost round, curled up dog, its neck split down the middle. The sheet, fallen to the ground, an abandoned veil, like a tragic bride's. He switched the light on and the magic vanished: the sheet lost its tragic character and the pillow resumed its identity as a simple, vulgar, forlorn pillow. In the goldfish bowl, his fighting fish emerged from the lethargic shadows and moved its blue fins as if ready to fly: except that its flight was an interminable circling around frontiers imposed by the roundness of the glass. "Rufino, I'm going to get you some company, but you'll have to love her like I do," said the Count and he tapped his nail on the transparent glass and the animal assumed an attacking stance.

He went back into the kitchen and looked at his coffee pot. The coffee had yet to gurgle. The Count leaned the palms of his hands on the small table and contemplated the clear sky under the full moon, at rest and drowsy after so many days of relentless gusts. In the distance he could see the English tiled roof of the barrio's castle built on the only hill in the place. Rufino the Count, his Granddad, had put some of those tiles in place more than seventy years ago. The fighting cocks had gone, but the castle and its red tiles survived. The smell of coffee warned him it had started to percolate, but he didn't want to mash sugar. He simply dropped five spoonfuls into the coffee pot and stirred. Waited for the song of percolation to turn into a splutter and switched off the burner. Filled a breakfast cup to the rim and put it on the table. Picked up the shirt he'd abandoned on the other chair and looked for a cigarette. On the table lay the notebook where he'd written down his obsessions over the last few days, as if in the pages of a diary: death, marijuana, forlornness and memories. The effort now seemed a foolish waste of time: he knew he'd never write again and couldn't stand reading those revelations that had no future. Two nights before, in that same chair, he'd had a happy dream brought on by the music Karina played. It was now an empty chair, like his punctured soul or fragile reservoir of hopes. He thought it was alarming how easily heaven and earth could combine to crush a man like a sandwich about to be chomped painfully. He sipped his coffee slowly, and tried to imagine how he'd get out of bed at dawn. Nobody knows what the nights of a policeman are like, he thought, anticipating he wouldn't have the strength to re-visit something that had lost all its novelty. As always, he regretted not having a supply of alcohol at home, but he'd never warmed to the frustrating monologue of the solitary drinker. In drink, as in love, you needed good company, he told himself, despite his onanist inclinations. But never drinking.

He stubbed out his cigarette in the bottom of his cup and went back to his bedroom. Put his pistol on the sideboard and his trousers dropped to the floor. Pulled them off with his feet. Opened the windows and switched off the light. He couldn't read. Could almost not live. He shut his eyelids tight and tried to convince himself that the next best step was to sleep, to sleep, not even dream. He fell asleep more quickly than he thought he would, and felt himself sinking into a bottomless lake, and dreamed he lived by the sea, in a house made of wood and tiles and loved a red-headed woman with small suntanned breasts and skin. In his dream he always saw the sea calm and golden against the light. In the house they roasted a red, shiny fish that smelled of the sea, and made love under the shower that soon disappeared to leave them on the sand, making love, until they fell asleep and dreamed happiness was possible. It was a long, muted, precise dream from which he woke painlessly, when the sunlight re-entered through his window.

Mantilla, 1992

286